Fray

Fray

Chris Carse Wilson

Harper
North

HarperNorth
Windmill Green
24 Mount Street
Manchester M2 3NX

A division of
HarperCollins*Publishers*
1 London Bridge Street
London SE1 9GF

www.harpercollins.co.uk

HarperCollins*Publishers*
Macken House, 39/40 Mayor Street Upper
Dublin 1, D01 C9W8, Ireland

First published by HarperNorth in 2023
This edition published in 2024

1 3 5 7 9 10 8 6 4 2

A catalogue record for this book
is available from the British Library

HB ISBN: 978-0-00-853920-7
PB ISBN: 978-0-00-853923-8

Printed and bound in the UK using 100% renewable electricity
at CPI Group (UK) Ltd, Croydon

MIX
Paper | Supporting
responsible forestry
FSC™ C007454

This book contains FSC™ certified paper and other controlled
sources to ensure responsible forest management.

For more information visit: www.harpercollins.co.uk/green

For Elaine and Niamh, for everything.

Chapters

Sometimes all you can do is climb to the peak of the nearest mountain and scream, at the top of your voice, 'Devil, Devil, Devil!'

That might buy you some more time to run.

This was the first note I read, not long after discovering the cottage he'd been hiding in for nearly a year. Or perhaps not hiding, but certainly hidden.

Dad disappeared shortly after Mum died, shortly after I drove him away. He took her death badly, but not in the usual sense. Dad didn't believe in the truth of it – he thought she was elsewhere, not gone but discoverable. He thought she was there to be found.

And I found, eventually, this near-derelict abandoned cottage, hidden in the forests and mountains of northern Scotland. Somewhere they used to go before I was born, but somewhere we never went as a family. A special place, but a hidden place even then.

Inside was a sea of writing, spread over every surface. Crude hand-drawn maps and ripped pieces of paper thrown everywhere. A giant jigsaw tipped out of its box.

She is near, and I can feel it. I have started to seriously explore now. To begin my search. There are layers here, fogs and clouds, sharp blades of light. Somewhere in there she is trapped.

There are endless miles and mountains, and in every weather they change. She may be here but not here, she may move with the light.

The police said no one owned the cottage, and it isn't marked on any maps. Deep inside a forest, hours and miles from anyone or anywhere, long since forgotten.

A squat pile of stones holding a simple roof over one solitary room. An empty fireplace, an old table and chair, a camp bed frame with no sleeping bag, and nothing else apart from all the paper. A smell of stale, still air inside, and heady pine resin outside. Some water had come down the chimney and under the door, but surprisingly little for the extremes of weather that cascade through these mountains.

Not quite a house, rather a shrine lost in a forest.

To start with, no one was sure where he was. Mum's funeral came and went, the rush of shared grief and strangers passed. And a few days later he went too, after our heated, burning words. My words. Quietly, coldly, with just a mountaineering bag and some basic outdoor clothing, he left. With a pair each of worn-out hiking boots and running trainers, he left.

I thought he would return within a few hours, maybe a day or two. No note, no calls, nothing but dead silence. When it became clear he had really gone I tried to look, I tried to find help. Bulky policemen sat awkwardly in my parents' front room, scratching into comically small notepads. They wore belts holding the tools of crime and capture: handcuffs and radios and more. Tools that were meaningless to me.

I assumed he had run to the Lake District, somewhere we had gone often as a family. A place of escape and adventure. Of walking and sunshine and family warmth, of woodsmoke carried on the frozen air. I looked south and he ran north.

It took me a while to catch up.

To cover ground once is not enough. To cover ground during day and night, and every weather, is essential.

But someone else is searching too. I must hurry.

It took almost nine months to find where he had gone. Months of grieving, fractured and doubled, certainty clouded and confused. Through a winter, spring, summer, and back to autumn again. Sifting through their home, with its new weight and sorrow, not knowing what to keep and what to throw away. How do you pack up and move on from a death and a disappearance? When does a silence become permanent, become sure?

I stopped and started, stopped and started. I drove to the Lake District and tracked old holiday homes, walked winding streets, watched the villages and fells swell with warm-weather visitors, then recede again. A great migration, but still nothing.

I tore through their cupboards and drawers, looking for anything that might suggest, that might explain. I turned over and over those final words, that guilt and weakness, the hot anger that pushed him away, pushed him too far. The strength of words, and their failure.

Finally, I came to a beaten cardboard box of old photograph albums, hiding under a pile of dusty curtains in their attic. Something from their early days, perhaps even their honeymoon. Yellowing images of hillsides, of views from peaks, and a pile of battered hillwalkers' maps, frayed along their folding lines, creases that spoke of rain and drying, of repeated opening and closing in the wet and the wind.

A photograph of Mum, glowing, standing outside a tiny cottage, slightly blurred as she turns to the camera, mid-laugh. She is surrounded by towering pines, stretching far above her. And on one map there was a single, simple dot. A mark to suggest the centre of everything. Somewhere you might run in anger, in pain, to discover and remember, or to pretend that nothing has happened.

Today I came upon the grand disused hotel, boarded up and rain-beaten. Collapsed and resigned, high on a hill.

Once it thrived with wealthy patrons looking to walk the land and destroy what they disturbed. To imagine Scotland, to play in pantomime tweed, and drink and shoot and kill.

Driving to the wilderness was both calm and crazed. A beautiful and manic trip through rolling countryside, feeling the land change as you climb higher, as hills grow to mountains, as nature becomes bigger and fiercer everywhere you look. I was driving towards a dot, towards an old photograph that told me nothing, chasing a desperate hope.

If not there, then where? I had scoured, searched, trailed everywhere else I could think of. I had nothing left to give and nowhere left to go.

It was close to impossible to find. A place to hide, miles and miles from anywhere, completely invisible from both inside and outside the forest, covered by a whispering canopy of evergreen needles.

I slowly drove along the rough, rutted track, fearing that my car would get stuck. I crawled over the bridged river, along the trail until it faded, disappeared, until I had to pick my way between trees, avoiding stumps and roots, then deeper and deeper, and then I arrived.

It was the photo from the attic, but with no one to be seen. No smiling, younger Mum, no Dad taking the picture, his back to the sunshine spilling through the trees. The forest was alive again, no longer faded and yellowed.

I found hope, after months of searching, after hours of driving, exhausted, always exhausted. Hope that lasted just long enough to run from the car, burst through the cottage door, expecting to find him sitting there, expecting tears and reunion and apologies, only to be met with paper piled upon paper. Inside me something tore further still.

Walking around, the outside matched the photograph but didn't. My eyes flitted from the faded colours to the uneven brightness of the wilderness. She looked so happy then, freckled, hair and sunshine almost merging into one, lean and athletic from years of movement, not thin and frail from death's sudden pull. The cottage looked barely changed, bar a carpet of moss silently creeping over its roof.

I looked around, I listened. No one could find this by accident. Perhaps that was the point.

At the hotel's front door, where bags would have been taken and Sirs and Ma'ams swapped for small handfuls of dirty coins, a lone CCTV camera stared. A metal box, fixed, unmoving, with a red eye looking for unwanted arrivals.

And at the other end? Someone watching over, or just an empty dummy with a light to scare away bored teenagers flirting with trouble and fire?

I stared at the light. A laser, pointing, accusing. I stared at the light and felt her trapped somewhere on the other side. Somewhere beyond. Watching and waiting.

Once I'd finally found it, I sat inside the cottage, silent and stuck. I tried to count the number of pieces of paper and couldn't. The weight of the hurt was too heavy.

But my guess would be a few thousand sheets and scraps. I counted a little over two hundred pages before it all became too much. Before sinking to the floor, as if weakened by thin air. Standing on the top of

Everest, gasping, grasping for breath, while sitting on a cold stone floor in a glen in Scotland.

There was no clear order to the pieces, nothing obviously connecting one to another. No dates or clues. Most were words calmly placed on the page, but still words that were rushing to escape. Some were sketches of mountainsides and peaks. A few were very basic maps, which seemed to link together some of the sketches. All was totally baffling, and perhaps still is.

I stayed, but never slept there. I couldn't. Too cold, too dark, too much noise roaming the forest outside, whistling through the warped window frames, roaring down the chimney. I stayed and wrote, wrote letters to Dad, wrote for the sake of writing, but always asking questions. Pleading and reaching out.

That was my grieving, my paper prayers for two lost parents.

I had no idea what I would find next.

Today the weather changed. Brightness drowned. The Devil is here now.

Dawn

1.

This is the start, day one. He must be here, there must be more than all those notes and this confused nonsense about a devil. I will stay for a week, find something, anything, tell the police, help them find him, then move on, bring everything back home. Everything, if not everyone.

The paper is still spread out, as I am not yet ready to move it. I can't. I tip-toe around piles, glancing at the pages on top, as I find a way from the door to the chair by the table. The door is thick and wooden, any paint long since darkened to the point of being unrecognisable. At the edges the wood is softening, damp creeping in, rot starting. The walls are thick stone, as rough inside as out, punctured by a small window on each side. At the back, facing the door, is an open fireplace.

There are no signs of food, plates or pans, and no rubbish. The fire-place is clean, with just a faint dusting of white ash that could be from yesterday or a decade ago. Water must have been brought from the nearby river that flows with steady force, a constant rush and rumble behind the trees.

It is tidy and empty, bar the fury of paper.

Where could he be? Where has he moved on to now?

She called to me today, from behind the wind and rain. I stepped outside and felt her closeness.

Grabbing clothes and shoes, I ran. Noting the wind, the weather, the time, the light – to record later – I ran.

Carefully holding the speed to chase and the need to remember.

I'm not sure how to write this all down, but I feel I must. At the moment nothing has shape. I need words to pin back the terror, to craft and mould it, to make it mine. Simple and placid and understood.

But I don't have words strong enough to do this, or to do it quickly. This will take some time.

I've read many things about grief, most of which feel alien. Poor translations of an unknown language, losing their kindness or connection. Something, however, has stuck firm.

Grief is not a wound, not a laceration to slowly heal, repair, and scar, leaving a white flesh reminder of damage now recovered from. Grief is change, or a symptom of it.

You do not recover from grief and return back to who and what you were before. You emerge new and different, though not necessarily better or improved. At the end you are someone else.

The light is casting moving shadows, dancing with the wind, rippling across the forest floor, the stone walls, the back of my hand.

Everything can be seen and heard. I can hear her. She is near.

I am staying in a tiny wooden cabin in an empty campsite on the shore of the nearest loch. An internet booking, a key in a lock-box, no other person to be seen. At this time of year no one wants to be here.

After reporting this lost cottage to the local police, I bought a heavy padlock to lock it, then came back to look again. Not mine to protect, but still I did.

When the police arrived they didn't seem to care either way, as nothing immediately pointed to where he actually is, or if he's even still alive. I felt like a nuisance to them, one older, one younger, both equally bored.

The cottage belongs to no one, they said, and is too far away from the popular mountains to ever be a bothy for walkers to shelter in. Then the notes were skimmed through and quickly dismissed as wild ramblings. I could feel their interest being lost to the silence.

They will search the glen, the loch, and have alerted the mountain rescue. They will look for his car but expect to find nothing. They urged me to leave, to go back home, back to somewhere safer.

After they left I sat for a long time inside the cottage, trying to imagine him here, and failing. I drank it all in.

For a long time, there was hope, uneven but blinding hope. The paper, so much paper. It must have taken him months, and there have only been months. He must be alive, he must be here, he must be?

Hope falters. It falters in silence, in questions asked and never answered. In a forest that surrounds and suffocates, that takes the light and keeps it from you. I have a week, nearly a week. I will read the notes, I will search.

The sunset comes, the day retreats. I am staying.

I must keep studying, to test and move closer to her.

I need to be rigorous and careful and thorough.

10.13am. Strong wind, easterly. Light rain. Cool.

Day three. I'm trying to build a routine, a way of understanding how to find him even if I understand nothing else. To wake at the campsite, in no more than a wooden pod where my feet touch one wall and my head another, to wash in the empty shower block, to fill up my water bottles and make sandwiches, to hurry back here and try again.

I can read it all, surely I can. A few hundred pages each day, quickly read. That must be possible. Just until I discover something helpful, to take to the police, to focus their search.

At first, I overlooked the notes at the end of most of the pages. Time, weather, occasionally other observations. No set format as such, but a rough impression of each moment.

After a while these additions came into focus. Patterns emerged. I can feel that Dad was trying to test and repeat, to find out how differences in the light and the weather affected his search for Mum.

He seems to have become obsessed with the idea that as well as being reachable, she was locked away. That at a certain moment he could find her, grab her, pull her back to this world. It's disorientating and heartbreaking to read. It opens up wounds I'm desperately trying to close, bringing me back to retching out tears, crying so hard my stomach muscles cramp, my jaw seizes.

It's also inconsistent and muddled. But it feels like he knows this too, that it's all part of the experiment. Of finding.

What I found shocked me. Nothing could have prepared me for this.

Trying again. I've been out already this morning, over the scree and some of the sharpest slopes, playing games with endless fake summits. It was bright, cool, and breezy, a wind of encouragement and comfort. But then something shifted.

I came back, rested, drank cold tea left from earlier, drank fresh hot tea, and watched the wind change its mind. Something snapped, a whiplash or about-turn, and it blew against itself. The brightness was lost to a deafening darkness.

This felt like a response, a rebuff, a laughing, scorning wind that knew I'd failed again, on another day, and wanted to mock me for it.

15

It knew where she was. It knows where she is. Something is playing with me, and senses my weakness and willingness to quit. My flesh and failure. I had to go back out, along the track, remembering that these are not the same hills. Everything has changed.

This is the first mistake everyone makes in mountains. This is why people die. You must show fear and respect, obey the gods that grant you entrance and decide whether you get to leave or not. That's the second mistake – assuming that leaving is assured, even if you quit partway. You have to show your fear. It isn't enough just to feel it. You have to display your respect or you will be punished, as I am again and again.

The rough track crests, rising and twisting, merging to forest floor and then to mountain. Feeling the wind throwing fat raindrops, sharpened to ice needles. Ignoring and breathing and rising up further and further.

The loose stones take over and everything slows. Step and slide. Move, breathe, move. Looking up I can remember being here just a few hours ago, though it all looks different now – glinting, sparkling rock disappeared to grey death. And now hard rain, changing again, polishing black to mountain silver.

Not up this time, to the high ridge, but along the other path and a little further down. To a hollow of huddled trees, scratched and battered by wild roaming deer. The bark riven by new antlers scraping away their soft outer flesh, shedding and marking territory. Dried velvet hangs, frayed against saplings that are now bare and unprotected.

And everything stops. Frozen. No wind. Nothing.

This is the closest I have come, but to what I do not dare to think. Nothing stirs. I stand and look around, slowly.

16

The sky erupts. Lights up. Lightning scratches down, landing back near the cottage, and thunder fills the air. It is not sound. It is the gods shaking with fury. Fear would have been staying back. Respect would have been waiting until tomorrow, not pouncing and returning on the same day. Their patience is limited and my desperation is not.

Clouds mass overhead, playground bullies acting for others. Calling and shouting, talking of knives and lessons and telling.

The sky explodes again. Lightning, thunder, darkness.

Breathe. Keep breathing to keep calm. To recover, to hold oxygen, to be ready to run again.

And then another flash of lightning. A brief glimpse, giving the world shape and depth for a moment.

The outline of a creature, standing upon the hilltop, a very short distance away, looking down on the hollow and the trees and me. Shapeless, shimmering. As if seen through burning heat, or made of it.

The Devil, lit in brilliant light, and then a blackout.

Breathe, breathe, breathe. Hold on and listen in the still and the silence. Listen for clue or footstep or loose rocks tumbling down the hillside. But nothing. Panic holding and rising. And still nothing.

Lightning strikes again. It has gone.

I am sitting now, but never chose to sit. I am trapped in place, not safe but steadying, waiting for my moment to escape as the light slowly fades in, as the darkness moves on to another hill, another glen, other terrors.

17

It feels like dawn, but is afternoon already. And I run, I run, I run. I run over rock and root, slide down scree. I throw myself off this mountain and curse gravity every step of the way. I fall, slide, scrape, bleed, recover a little, and run, faster and faster and faster.

I reach the cabin and collapse and know that I have woken the gods, I have found the Devil, I have begun to find her.

9.27am. Bright. 12.11pm. Dark.

I understand the depth of his despair. They were everything to each other, and her death was quick and brutal and totally bereft of dignity. Her body failed and she had nowhere to go.

We watched instant decay arrive with no warning, and in a matter of weeks she disappeared. A recurring pain, some odd symptoms doctors were never quite able to pinpoint. Pathetically quiet signals of our own personal hurricane.

But his response to the despair, and these endless, infuriating notes are too much. Gods and devils and pointless, childish madness. Why a devil? He had no faith, no religious guilt hanging over him. It's such an odd reference for someone who didn't believe.

I keep hoping that I'll find something sensible, a clue, another location he may have moved to, but it's just not here. He is here, but there is so little of him. He is disappearing too.

I try not to think of him inside this old, dark cottage, wildly putting his thoughts down on paper. His panic, his anger, the swirling confusion. But I try not to think of him out there either.

He was alone, his mind spiralling and inventing, building layers of imagination to hide everything that had really happened. I am torn to pieces by this.

I am trying to find him, in the pages and the mountains, to hold him and console him, to say sorry. I am looking, for his sake and mine. But I can see nothing of the scale of it. I still can't see the peak. I had thought I could do this, overcome this, discover something for the police, then grab him and leave. I thought it could be simple, but it can't.

Mum died, we grieved, we fought, he ran. I'm left archiving a paper trail of his mental collapse, searching for clues that might not be here, or might be waiting on the very next page.

Today was dull. I woke early, to check, to start again, to retrace steps.

But it's all gone and different.

7.12am. Cloud, dull, grey.

I must try to find this hollow, this imagined place of the devil, even if the very thought is sickening. I want to look away, but maybe there's a clue I can find? Could he even be there, waiting, returned?

19

Heading out from the cottage, it's a hard walk up a long, rough slope. I can feel the trees fading behind me, the horizon stretching out further and further as I climb.

This feels wrong. I am full of his words and fears, of his unhappiness and my own. But I must go on.

Reaching the edge of the hollow, I slide down rolling scree to the bottom. At its base it's a little bigger than the cottage and could easily be overlooked. A few old ragged trees desperately reach for the sky, warped by the wind even with the protection from the severe slopes on each side. It is darker and colder here.

There is nothing to see. I can picture everything he wrote about, can see how he would have been craning his neck to look up to the lip, that point where the earth seems to suddenly collapse.

There is no Dad or devil. I want to burn the whole world to the ground.

I can't come back here again. It's too much.

I followed yesterday exactly, the afternoon of fire and darkness, but there was nothing.

The Devil has moved on. I must too.

4.32pm. Dry.

2.

I am here chasing Dad, but overlooking Mum. I am reading of his seeking, following him following her, but in this I know I am starting to forget her.

This feels uncomfortable and wrong, but it is easy to be swept away by the grief that is nearer, brighter, even just simply louder and more confusing. What takes your attention, takes it away from you.

What happened to her is awful, but understood. There were the hissing, bleeping hospital machines. There were hazed days and nights, merging to one, sudden yet lasting forever. There was a cremation, in an angular concrete building set in soft woodland, light flooding through skylights. A faint memory of being there before, much younger, to mourn someone I have now forgotten, someone else I have misplaced.

I may be in the mountains, but I'm still sitting on a hard wooden pew as the hymns fade, the reluctant voices and half-caught throats rising in cautious song. She would have hated this, I thought. Actually, she would have laughed hard, if she were able. That expectation, that assumption she still went to church. A service for those around her but not for her.

At this point my memories of Mum are stuck somewhere. I can get no further back than the crematorium, the folded cardboard orders of service, with a front cover photograph I knew she wouldn't have picked and am still not sure who did. There remains a gap, a gap I cannot bridge, so I don't.

It is morning, day four. I drive back to the hidden cottage and look away. I listen to the rain falling on the roof and look away.

Coldly moving on, trying to forget, looking for the easiest way up the mountain that keeps away from the hollow, from those memories, from the burning.

Finding that every direction takes you nearer to what you are trying to avoid.

9.41am. Clouding.

We left after the strange procession of handshakes and condolences, of being on display, mourners passing by, as if for our approval. To be seen and noted, to be an official part of the day. A crowd lingered, held together loosely, slowly losing its shape. Too slowly.

I remember the hurt and the overwhelm, the well-wishing that kept coming and coming, the feeling of suffocating in others' kindnesses. I remember wanting to step away, needing to, but any face you looked away from brought you to another. And another. To caring and love, but in a moment when you needed silence.

And in that moment the woodland was alive, rich with birdsong, ringing clear on a cold, bright day, the crematorium chimney lightly smoking far above our heads. I wanted nothing more than to listen to the bird calls, to walk in those woods and be lost, to connect back to Mum and her love of nature and identifying hidden creatures by their sounds alone. I strained to hear their clashing, overlapping melodies in the background, strong and shifting, but distant. They lay behind the low conversations that hummed across the bare, flat grass.

Dad and I held each other, frozen together, unsure who was the adult and who was the child, unsure where we could go from there. The birds sang, knowing nothing of this.

Forgetting, forgetting, forgetting. I am hiding from the Devil.

It is real and happening now. I must move. To be ahead, to stay ahead, to catch up.

To the mountain, to find something in myself. Poring over maps, contour lines and suggestions, a flattened world waiting for me, waiting for me to find her.

There is so much mountain to check, rock by rock by rock.

2.01pm. Wind rising.

I'm only managing a few dozen pages each day. They hurt to read and each piece of paper feels slower, heavier than the last. The cottage is dark inside, with tiny windows and trees blocking any sunshine that might help, might ease the strain.

I try to read the notes from a distance, to let go of any expectation that a page needs to follow a page, that sentences need to be finished, that anything can be clean and neat and simple, but it is impossibly hard to do this. Whatever you try, you are pulled back. Wherever you lean and look, there is a gravity, holding you, tugging you, expecting more of you.

Perhaps the pieces are no more than that. Perhaps there are no stories that conveniently link one thing to another, no clues I can report back, nothing that will help the police find him. Perhaps it is all slipping away.

I think of his mind like this, as if it was fragmenting the more he walked and explored, the more he hallucinated and imagined. Bringing more and more words together doesn't necessarily improve anything.

From gap to gap, never fully able to rest, to find real peace. I am trying to look in a mirror by gathering shards of broken glass.

Every day I try to write something of my own too, to take the smallest step forward in words, closer to Dad. It often doesn't work, or doesn't work well. I am writing on the edge of a cliff, knowing the sheer drop is there, but I'm too scared to look closely.

I keep my pages carefully separated from his, in small notebooks, stuffed inside my jacket. I keep them close to me, so we can't become confused.

HIDING

HIDDEN

FIRE

DARKNESS

LISTEN

As the day dragged on I needed to get out, to be in nature, surrounded and reassured by it. I needed to forget why I'm here, at least for a moment.

At this time of year the glens are a shock of orange, brown, and burgundy. The grasses and bracken are changing colour, small patches of deciduous trees turning and losing leaves, naked in waves of evergreen forest. And it is all torn through by the dark grey terror of the mountains, and by lochs and lochans, at once still and glassy and stirred and rippling. Brushed by the wind, broken. Always moving, never stopped.

The weather here has a suddenness, a violence. It can change so quickly and with such force. That can mean waiting an hour or two for bad weather to pass until a walk or climb becomes possible, or it can mean safety being taken away from you without notice.

Today was bright and clear, very little weather on the horizon, no signs of anything threatening coming in. But this didn't last. I'd walked up the ravine between two tall peaks, thinking about glaciers carving out this great landscape, slowly grinding rock, picking gigantic stones with ease and softly placing them far, far away.

From higher up I could see the incredible speed that clouds rush through here. Layers upon layers, filtering the sunlight which splashes where it can, suddenly warming, suddenly cooling. A sharp shower of rain followed, then abruptly stopped. The sun returned and almost instantly I was dry again. The wet ground steamed despite the cold, all of the rocks now slick and shining bright.

The mountains are scoured by erosion, with scree settling in the crevices. Long lines of grey running down, an echo of water passing through. There are waterfalls that appear here only at certain times of year, frothing noise and whiteness, crashing to the ground, then gone again. Gone, except for their scars.

Here everything is massive, and nothing is as you expect it, as Dad said. The mountains become more forbidding, more resistant as you start hiking, running, or climbing up them. They push back, gravity feeling heavier, harder with every step.

And as I pushed on, the ravine flooded with cloud. Thick milky air, textureless. I could see nothing beyond my hands and feet. All sound softened and smoothed, dulling the hard crunching of my boots over the loose stones.

I sat where I stood, on rough broken stones, knowing that moving through cloud can so easily lead to distraction and confusion, to unseen edges. I sat and waited for the wind to carry it away, for the light to burn back through.

Resting, to try to rest, to find some peace. It is all cold and fire, never between, never settled.

The mountains are frozen, snow over the tops, hiding in gaps, barely touched by the weak winter sunlight. The snow will lie in corries for months now, long after it was laid.

I went out today but stumbled early on, caught by ice, a glistening layer laid over rock. Not looking, not paying attention.

Cursing myself, feeling the pain, knowing this might take days to pass, for me to recover. I carried on, slower, always looking, always trying to look.

5.12pm. Hard cold.

Day five. I am sitting in the cottage and trying to understand him here, writing furiously, spreading these pages across the table and the floor. I imagine him warm by the fire in winter, or with the door open at the height of summer, as I sit in my coat, hat, and gloves, each breath a fading cloud.

I didn't see it at first, but among all the noise in these writings and scribblings and smudged charcoal maps something is missing: I am utterly absent.

27

I pushed him away at his weakest moment, and now I am invisible. Now I know I deserve to be.

I do not exist, and yet I know I am the only one left. That I must be.

The Devil is here and she is here.

It has her, it cannot have her. She belongs to no one.

She is here, but I can't find anything useful, anything that can help.

She is here, but I am not.

2.56pm. Spitting rain.

It is less than two days until I have to leave for work again. There is a mountain of paper left, with barely any read and even less understood. I have protected myself from the truth, but there are no clues, there is nothing I can give to the police. He has disappeared, regardless of what he left behind.

They were here together. I know this, but know so little of it. I hold the photograph and try to recreate that ageing picture again, imagining everything that was going on before and after, in front of and behind the camera.

It looks like summer, much warmer than now. Mum is in a short-sleeved top, bright yellow against the browns and greens that surround her, with hair messed by the wind and loosely tied back. She looks slightly pink in her cheeks from too much sun, from the sting of wind on a mountainside, from eating outdoors. There is an ease to her that I recognise from our holidays together, from before the illness. Those trips from childhood, sand whipped by wind, pealing seagulls, eating hot chips in the salt air. But each time I get stuck on a detail. I find something missing.

I walk around inside the cottage, lost among the words. The piles of paper cluster and I can step through them, or follow an almost unbroken line around the edge of the stone floor. I wonder what this might have been when it was first built – a single room, a single fireplace, possibly for a family, more likely for someone managing a hunting estate, keeping nature in check for the wealthy.

Mum and Dad must have rented it when they first came here, or perhaps it was already abandoned and was simply extra shelter on a camping trip to the Scottish wilderness. I guess I'll never know.

Another day ends. I lock the door and leave, again.

I found where the lightning hit. Behind the cottage, hidden from the door and the windows, on the opposite side to the mountain.

A tree, burnt and cut through, that traced a violent collapse and took another, smaller tree with it. It still smelled of burning.

It smelled of threat.

3.27pm. Cold.

3.

Day six. I have until tomorrow to pack everything and leave. I feel frantic, distracted, but know there is nothing here for me. I have to grow up and get on.

I drove out of the glen to a village about twenty miles away, and bought flat-pack cardboard storage boxes from the tiny Post Office that doubles as the only shop within an hour of here. I left the shop far emptier and the owner looking more than a little confused by my purchase. We smiled, spoke of the weather, but little more.

I really could not have begun to explain why I was packing up so much stuff, or what I was packing. I am glad he didn't ask.

I need to make a study of the skies, of the light, of the wind and weather. I need to think multiple steps ahead, and be planning and waiting, not reacting after everything has changed. By then it is all too late.

Today confirmed this, deep in the forest. It was a day for walking – legs tired and sore from days of scrambling up rocks, looking for cracks and caves and crevices but finding none.

I spent the whole day on edge. I walked for hours and hours, moving into parts of the forest the bright light doesn't seem to touch. I didn't have my torch as it wasn't even lunchtime when I started, but that felt like more and more of a mistake as I went.

But still I went. I had a feeling of stalking prey, of being permanently several steps behind. I picked up the pace, moving as lightly as I could over the rolling forest floor, dressed underfoot with dried larch needles and pine cones and animal excrement turned furry and white.

As I moved faster I became noisier, giving up on the idea of pursuing some wounded animal, as many people in these forests and mountains have before. I moved instead in search of anything interesting or different, thinking about how this place would look in darkness, in rain, with the wind ripping through the treetops and casting broken shadows far below.

A fallen tree, some animal burrows, but little more.

10.57am. Bright, cold. Wind changing.

I'm not sure how to start packing the cottage away, but know I have to be quick. I've been throwing myself at a shapeless, shifting problem, and nothing has happened. Every day I have shivered in the old stone cottage, too scared to light a fire, scared of tricking myself into feeling comfortable here. Into thinking that any of this is normal.

Each page feels slight, almost weightless, but they all cut deeply. They shine a light on the pain that is already there, that I am trying so hard to obscure, to ignore.

He didn't mean it to be like this, of course. He was writing for himself, documenting and striving, experimenting all the time. I try to stay focused on this: that he needed to do it. That I shouldn't be angry, even if I am.

To look at the pages is to remember Mum, is to long for Dad, is to wonder where he could be, what fate he met. I feel torn in so many directions. From a distance I may look whole, human, with a body that moves and breathes and takes up space. Up close I am a cloud. You could walk straight through me, or watch pieces of me blow away on the breeze.

The boxes need to be built, folding and tucking in tabs that connect, ready to be filled. It's like the summer I spent in our local library archive, handling old books, wearing protective gloves, showing reverence as if performing ritual and sacrifice. I can't work out if that should apply here too. Part of me feels a need for solemn respect, but I know there's nothing to be gained from reading any more of this.

I'm stretching at the very edges of my compassionate leave from work, at the limits of other people's patience. At some point painful normal life must begin again, away from mountains and madness, with awkward colleague reassurances and workplace whispers.

I start quickly, trying not to think too much about anything. As the papers seem to have no order, I take piles as they lie, swiftly placing them into the boxes, numbering them in the order I fill them. I know I don't have long.

CHASING

CHASING

STALKING

FINDING

Packing up was always hard for my family, something none of us were very good at. Holidays were bright, beautiful things, but the beginnings and the ends were often tense and traumatic. No matter how much time was planned for checking and sorting there was always a rush, a painful moment of losing control. Sometimes I wondered if the rest of the holiday was worth it.

Usually it was. We had wonderful trips, invariably linked in some way to coasts or peaks, though never here, never these mountains. Mum craved the adventure away from her long hours as a teacher, and Dad was always thrilled to support her. He would have done anything for her, whether he wanted to or not. Often it felt that, despite his own love of running and climbing, he was only pursuing these things for her joy. That was everything to him.

Now I don't know what I'm doing, what I'm packing up. I feel a compulsion to collect and keep these papers, like they need to be

33

contained. Not as evidence, but as protection. Protection against whatever lurks here.

The more I read, the more dangerous they feel. But quick, I must be quick.

I watched the sun rise today, watched it all. I climbed one of the smaller peaks as it was growing lighter, as the sky starts changing well before the sun breaks through the horizon. A shorter gap in winter, longer in the summer. Slower.

A memory came back, of years ago, travelling much further north than here for the longest day of the year, when the sun barely sets. Feeling this as a sense of possibility, as twisting the rules of what a day is, of what it can be. It felt joyful and reckless. She swam in the sea in the middle of the night, laughing at the lightness, at the absurdity of it, and I refused. I don't even remember why, but she laughed at me too. I wish I'd swum.

Cloud lay across the glen today, below my feet, as the sky above turned to pinks and golds. The sun burned orange and fierce, shimmering over the horizon, boiling the water that it touched, forcing me to look away. My face warmed.

9.07am. Bright, tired.

A few boxes done, many more to go. It is frozen dry outside, winter nearing. Each page pulls at me, begging to be read, as if it will be the one that reveals all, that gives the clue, that points me to him. But they also take me back, back to a time that's simpler, easier to rest in. I want to be taken away.

We moved house only once as a family. Once, and never again. I was young, not long started school, and our flat was too small. A young couple's home had become a family home, had become tiny and cramped, busy and noisy. We needed more rooms, a garden, some breathing space.

I don't remember much of this, but have heard the story so many times that it feels like my memory. Dad packing our life into boxes, labelling everything, organising and editing our belongings. Creating a structure entirely unlike what he's left me here. Mum was much more relaxed, but no doubt happy to let Dad continue however he was most comfortable.

What I do remember was how I felt on the day itself, panicking as loud men, big men, took away all of our things, shouting and stamping. I'm sure they were just doing their job but it was terrifying to a child, watching our home being swiftly stripped to its bones, blank and lifeless. Empty but for the three of us, closing the door on the departing removal van.

Then into the car to follow in its wake, not travelling far but the journey still feeling momentous, impossible. We got stuck in terrible traffic, hearing about an accident on the local radio, sitting and waiting, cars crawling, drivers getting angry, impatient.

Later, I've been told, we got to the police cordon, the flashing blue lights. That point where everyone slows to look, despite themselves. I think I remember the lights. It was our van, crumpled, on its side by a roundabout, having been struck by a car driving far too fast. A young man, a schoolboy really, who had recently passed his driving test. Recently passed, then quickly dead, nearly killing the van driver too. He lost control.

We arrived at our new house with no belongings except a single suitcase of clothes, a few small bags, and a record player. Mum's record player that she cherished so much. We sat in our empty home, the home that they would never leave, where they both lived until recently, with nothing but a few useless possessions and cold shock.

Days later our boxes arrived, some bent, some flattened. Opening our things that had been packed so carefully, for Mum and Dad to sift through what was broken and what was not. They would tell this story with sadness, wondering how you unpack your belongings once they have been changed by the world going on around them. They told this story when I was learning to drive.

I don't know if this was the reason they never moved again, but from that day packing and leaving always had an extra weight. Now another weight has been added.

I look at the paper again. Before, I hadn't noticed how the piles have their own contours, their own ridges and peaks. Without realising, he has created a mountain range inside the cottage, where the heaps tower over one another, shaping valleys between. When the sunlight sneaks in it casts shadows.

It is mid-afternoon already. I've barely achieved anything. I must stop thinking, stop remembering.

Where is the difference? I'm struggling with this. It can be easy to see sometimes, obvious, too obvious, or it can be so slight as to disappear in a moment.

The difference between air and light, between warming and cooling, between finding and fleeing.

I am searching, but am I finding?

3.31pm. Inside.

Exhaustion is creeping. I'm tired from the strain in my jaw, my arms. My legs are constantly tensed, feeling anxiety clawing and scratching. A short break? I can stop, for a moment, but then need to speed up. I will.

His writing can be incredibly varied. All focused on one thing, but from so many different points of view as to bear no relation from one note to another. Randomly jumping from thought to thought.

It seems he was searching in the forest and the mountains, and searching in the words too. Not knowing the words until they started to spill out, not knowing the mountains until he began to climb.

This idea that nothing is the same from one moment to the next occurs over and over, in so many ways. That the mountains change in light and rain, but maybe also that the words change with the weather, with his weather, with all the confusion and turmoil he brought to them.

37

I am changing too, slowly, but not in a good way. I feel an anger that bubbles, getting nearer to the surface every day. He is here, lost somewhere, alive or dead, and more than anything else, more than loss or fear or worry, I feel rage. I am angry at the selfishness, the indulgence, the imagined devil. I sit in the cottage and boil.

Is that wrong? I don't know. I am alternating between anger at him and anger at myself. At him for leaving, at me for my sharp words, those poorly chosen words that packed a bag for him and quietly closed the door.

My noise and his silence.

I have lost several days now, and today barely made it out before sunset.

The bleak cold of the past few weeks disappeared almost the moment I became sick. I have spent three, maybe four days inside and feverish, while outside the sun shone furiously and scared the clouds away. The weather was mocking my illness.

As soon as I began to move again, the clouds returned and spat at me.

I went out late, slowly, retracing my steps from the last trip, but very cautiously. I didn't want to stray too far with night falling. I still haven't brought myself to explore properly after the sun sets.

I tell myself it's to save energy, that there is still so much to experiment with during the day, but I know these are lies. I am terrified, as at night I have no control. Darkness belongs to the Devil.

3.19pm. Cold, cloud.

DARKNESS

HIDING

DARKNESS

NOW

It is almost dark now. I'm packing the final pages and can barely make out what they say. My fingers are numbed, slowing the picking and packing, and I keep dropping the paper. Frustration building upon frustration.

I am assuming at this point that he is dead, that he must be, probably through a reckless climb in terrible weather or – God forbid – falling from a knife-edge ridge at night. Grieving, again. A body will be found some day by a climber, another adventurer embarking on a simpler, saner trip. A horror for them, but a clearer end for me.

The boxes are full now, no paper left lying out. I feel sick and drained. The cottage looks clearer, emptier, more ordered, but this has brought no calmness or relief. Each page, each movement has ratcheted up my anxiety at roaming an unknown forest, searching for someone I've lost. A tension with no release.

I am left with a corner of the cottage piled high with heavy cardboard cubes. I've completed something sad and important, but have no one to tell about it.

No one but the creatures stirring in the forest as night falls. People talk of the silence of wilderness, but only if they've never been here. It is loud and unpredictable. The trees grind like rusted metal and rustle like water, birds shriek, animals burst into flurries of hunting or fleeing. Everything is stirring and waking.

I just need to leave. I just need to sleep.

4.

I woke with a shock, slumped in the hard wooden chair at the cottage table. The only furniture here bar the camp bed – his bed – which I can't bring myself to even sit on.

I had vowed never to sleep here, never to be here past nightfall. I'd always hated forests at night, as he did.

But I slept the whole night, heavy with exhaustion, with weakness. I was woken by pale sunlight. The boxes had fallen, but I'd heard nothing of this. I'd stacked them in such a state, I told myself, that I must have made a mess of it. They were so heavy that one falling and bringing the others with it was entirely likely. From some of the boxes the odd piece of paper had tumbled, though surprisingly few.

I righted the boxes that had fallen, putting them together on the floor, and collected the loose pages in my hands.

I felt hot sweat on my face and neck, and the cold rush of nausea swelling inside. I hadn't read any of these before and they felt like a twisted joke, played by someone watching. Someone hunting.

Coincidence, I told myself. Be rational, be calm, breathe. Remember Dad, remember Mum. They always said the same thing, smiling, at times of shock or panic or fright: breathe, breathe, breathe. Then take whatever happens next.

But what I was looking at made no sense. I dropped them all.

Don't run. Don't pack. Don't hide the pages.

I stared, then bolted. My old trainers were already on and I ran out of the door, not locking it, just slamming and escaping. I needed to move and flee and be gone from that place.

But I didn't go for my car, even though the keys were in my jacket pocket. I went for the forest, for the mountains, to run this out of my system. To feel breath and pain, to find release in panting exhaustion, to let the wind tear through me and leave nothing behind.

I wasn't sure I'd ever go back, ever go back anywhere.

Why would I? Where would I?

I am not gone. Mum is not gone.

We are here. We are hidden.

I ran, but not as I've ever run before.

This was something completely new. Raw. Desperately running away from impossibility, from fear, from looking too closely at the sun and feeling it burn into your retinas. A force so overwhelming that flesh can do nothing but turn away.

Step upon furious step. Biting at air, not breathing. A scream turned into motion.

I looked the wrong way. The Devil found me.

Running, running, always running.

I ran from the cottage, from the words, from the person I'm trying to find.

I wanted to run forever.

CHASING

CHASING

CHASING

I sprinted, blood and adrenaline thundering inside my skull. I stumbled over roots and sucked for air, with no rhythm to my footsteps or my breath.

For a moment I stopped. Deep in the forest, I'd carved circles around the cottage for an hour or more, at a safe distance. Everything else was still.

The words from the pages were shouting at me. His handwriting, definitely. Same plain paper. Same soft, dark pencil, but everything else was different. His writing before looked composed, even when the thoughts were wild and could not be held in one place. These words were erratic, scratched. Written at speed, in panic.

It struck me: he didn't have enough time to write. He stole those words, the time to create the new notes. They were written after he left. They were written without being allowed.

And I started moving again, this time with purpose, putting more distance between myself and the cottage. I went out of the woods, up one of the gentler slopes, keeping well away from that dark hollow. I needed to get high enough up to stop and look back over everything, to feel more control.

I reach a viewpoint of sorts and sit on a cold rocky ledge. It is raining. I hadn't noticed.

Please, please, help.

What's going on? I could be imagining this, I must be. There is no other way. It's beyond belief that he would play a trick so cruel, to be hiding and watching. To be waiting for this moment. Or that anyone else could be so accurate, so cutting with their words.

44

This is truly enough. For a moment I wish I was dead too, like Mum is, like Dad must be. Something to end this, whatever this is.

I fear I have cracked. I am clearly unwell. I have read about counselling, about professional help, about how modern and fine it is to be anything but fine. An illness or illnesses to be treated, to be recovered from, or at least moved past. I need to start moving past.

I sit for a long time, crying, then slowly get to my feet. The rain has eased and some of the cloud has shifted. In the distance other peaks reveal themselves, brilliantly lit, crashing down to a road that traces the edge of the sea. Silent cars so small I can barely see them.

Running isn't possible any more. I am tired beyond myself. I take slow steps down and try to breathe in time, try to feel the cold air coming in, holding and warming, before giving it back out in tiny misting clouds. Breathe, breathe, breathe. Some sort of rhythm is coming back to me, and I am thinking a little more clearly now. Breathe, breathe into it, I tell myself. Please.

Think of somewhere else, before all this, before here.

I first started running when I was young and awkward, just as my body was changing and everything was becoming uncertain, exciting, and terrifying.

Mum and Dad both encouraged me, gently. School running was miserable, a torture of thick winter mud and summer sports day humiliation, of performance and display, but actual running was something quieter and softer. It was pure private freedom.

It took me a while to understand this, as at the start it was all pain and discomfort. But within a few weeks everything began to ease, some of it quickly, some more slowly. The breathlessness took another few lamp-posts to hit, my cramping muscles failed to bite with as much force as last time. Building and building, making something new of myself.

Soon I discovered that running wasn't really anything to do with speed. Some people may move fast, which must be wonderful, but for many, many others it's a question of finding your rhythm, and then relentlessly appreciating how it repeats. Listening, not forcing it, respecting and loving how your body moves. Even, simply, that it can move like this when so many others cannot.

My foot catches on a rock, stirring me from the memory. Enough is enough. This must end, I never should have stayed. Safety is away from here, as forests and mountains are dangerous in so many ways. I have to go in, get the boxes, pack the car, padlock the cottage, leave. Leave and start to move on.

I am resolute. Whatever is happening, I am strong. I am.

With each step my certainty grows the tiniest amount. As the miles roll by, through undergrowth and forest cover, my resolve turns to solid stone. I am decided and cannot be turned back: this has been an experience beyond horrific. I am ill, following Dad's illness and Mum's illness. Theirs each killed them. Mine will not.

As I near the cottage, all is exactly as I left it. The door is shut, unlocked but firmly closed. I saw no one while I was away, and can see no one now. I look around, as if for the first time, scanning for any movement, any suggestion of another person, but remind myself that this lost, empty cottage is almost impossible to find. It was almost impossible for me to find, and I was looking, I wanted to find this so badly. But still I feel watched.

Many people in areas this remote don't lock their doors anyway, I tell myself. I live with city fear, so have never understood this. Is it pride, or complacency? Or something warmer and unknown to me when community is strong and everyone is known to everyone else, generation upon generation?

I am still not calm, but I am resolute. I am leaving, in the time it takes me to pack and turn a key one last time.

I will leave. I will.

But I come back to another note, sitting on top of the first.

It wasn't there before. It can't be here now.

I cry out. The stones crumble.

I didn't mean to scare you.

Read the other notes. Explore the mountains.

The Devil is there, and we are too.

I can't write any more. I love you.

5.

I am lost and lonely beyond all imagination. No family left, trapped deep inside a wild forest by mountains and fictional monsters, and stuck with a ridiculous puzzle. It's the breathless moment after life-changing bad news, or the frozen time waiting by a hospital bed. Nothing stirs, the air sits solid, we all slow and stop.

The initial panic has ebbed and I'm cautiously looking around. If these notes have been left, surely he is here? I look inside and outside, but nothing. No footprints, nothing changed, nothing disturbed. Pausing, I take a deep breath and listen. Nothing but the rustle and creak of a forest shaped by wind.

Whatever is going on, I'm persisting with writing some of this down. There's much that I'm missing as well, but I need to capture at least some of it, as soon as I can. Each word lets me take a step forward, piece something together, or lets me reassure myself a little. There is no one else left to whisper calmly to me.

There is no one here, and there's no one back home either. Even if I had a sense of who to call in a moment like this, mobile phones are useless here. Flashing rectangles, connecting to nothing and no one. Something many novice walkers discover in these mountains at the worst possible moment.

The last note was less rushed than those before. It reads very oddly, but it's the immediacy that has me spinning still. He was saying sorry, responding to a note that was itself responding to me trying to leave. Every part of this is impossible. I want to laugh and dismiss it all, but it has sunk a hook deep into me. I'm caught swimming in the currents, stuck underwater. I can see nothing above.

I sit and drink some water from my bottle. I can't remember when I last did that. My throat feels sandpaper rough.

I need to find a starting point, a viewpoint from which it all begins to make sense.

I came here, I stayed too long, I read too much. I packed up the piles of madness, fell asleep, woke to a note from nowhere, fled, then returned to another. I know I should leave, have to leave tomorrow, but maybe I try what he suggests. Maybe I should start reading again. Maybe I have no choice.

Is he in the words? Is he in the mountains? Are they? Mum is dead, surely dead. I was there, I know this. I watched the casket being taken behind a curtain, I felt the solemn music swelling, the undercurrent of sobbing all around. I stood in the cold, I heard that birdsong. I sat in my car for a long time afterwards, alone, watching the chimney above the crematorium.

I pick up the first box I packed, marked in blue pen with a numeral 1. I lift the cardboard lid, take the top page, and brace myself to start again. Eyes open.

We are past the winter solstice now, and the sunrise comes marginally earlier and the sunset slightly later.

Just a minute or two each way, each day. Nothing to notice in the moment but over time a thawing, something you feel rather than watch.

7.52am. Still night.

This must have been written not long after he first arrived here, after my anger at his calmness, at him grieving silently on the inside. That the outside said he didn't love her, didn't care that we hadn't been able to save her. I remember that feeling and the shame that followed. I want to forget it all.

But I must remember, I need to. I will keep coming back. I will keep reading, for now, to see what else I can find, giving myself another small pile of paper to get through each day, sorting boxes into read and not-yet-read. To see if I can settle, at least a little, to recover from everything that is happening and cannot be happening.

I can see why people are drawn here, and perhaps always have been. It is thrill and challenge, pure beauty and brutal indifference.

It means nothing to the mountain if you live or die, if you fail to pack a compass or a safety whistle. The forest doesn't hear you huffing up a mild slope, or have any view on the years you've wasted sat, screen-bound, your body and mind melting away. We are nothing to the wilderness. We are irrelevant.

Against that we can forge ourselves. Back before, when everything was complete and together, we both needed to seek out these self-imposed difficulties. Without struggle everything becomes fuzzy, as if life is slipping out of focus. It is endless, which is both the joy and the challenge.

We always came to places like this. It was something that drew us together from the very earliest moment. That exhilarating rush of finding someone who understands and shares your tiny passions, who has them cast deep inside too. To connect like that is blinding. I don't think it can be described to anyone who hasn't experienced it, like trying to explain how burning skin feels to someone who's never seen fire.

That, I think, is love.

8.01am. Cool, dry.

Most of his writing lasts no more than a single side of a single page. A few entries are very, very long, or seem to be: they are often jumbled and the faint thread of meaning from page to page has long since been lost. Sometimes I chance on pages that are in order, but more often than not I hit a dead end. Breathing in mid-sentence, pausing for words that never come.

The tension between his neat writing and his words tells stories of dread. The pages pulse. They show him fighting with a compulsion, a speed, trying to balance maintaining control with letting go. It's like he was falling down a mountainside, kicking back against gravity, pretending he could decide what happened next.

I imagine him trying to get everything down before the words dried up and were lost, his scattered mind struggling against the need to order and categorise. Forces in opposition, and him caught in between.

I'm calming a little now. Sitting at the table, in the wooden chair, I know I should stay here longer, should finish this properly. But I hope it's more out of respect than searching for my lost parents.

My parents are dead. My parents are dead. I repeat this to myself, silently and endlessly. How much I believe it changes with the wind.

Today was early. I am starting to feel settled here, which worries me. I need urgency, I need to be restless and moving. There is no time for scenery and glorious light, for playing with shadows. All are tricks of the Devil.

Up early, climbing high. I've been stuck in the forest for too long and I feel like I've found very little. There are a few lower routes I follow, but down at the glen floor I feel small. You can only see so far. I need to understand everything from another point of view.

A few of the climbs I avoid still. Too much scree, loose stones sliding over each other, drawing me back down the mountain as I push up. The rattling sound of tiny rocks falling far, far below, and the dead silence when they stop. Better to stay on the tracks worn by countless steady foot-steps than risk a fall.

Climbing is feeling a little easier, I am getting some strength back. Less wheezing. Lighter.

Over a low crest, then up again to one of the taller peaks. Below are treetops and wispy, rolling cloud, cut through by golden glass lochs with unseen depths. This is ancient beauty and at this time of day it is all mine.

But I have to check myself. She isn't waiting back at the mountain foot for me, stirring from happy sleep. There will be no coffee steaming on the cottage table, no morning of reading and long silences between two people in love. No memories to share, of before, like before. There is no one to tell stories to when I return.

I must stay focused. Everything around me is a distraction, the Devil's voice calling out.

She is here, she is here, she is here.

6.37am. Bright, cold, dry, wet.

I've settled now in a small rented house on the edge of a cluster of buildings that isn't quite a village. No shop, no pub, nothing to stop for.

Settled, or been forced to settle, I can't decide. Perhaps the difference doesn't matter, at least not to me. Not when I am always lost and words on a page can't even be trusted.

The few houses here are neat, grey, and lonely, about ten miles from the forest's edge and even further from the collapsing cottage. I've given up on returning home for now and have taken extended, unpaid leave from work. I think they expected this, were even relieved by it. A separation, but only for so long. I know I will have to return at some point.

I feel like tracing the changes in the writing would help me understand more of why he came here, and what happened in the run-up to his final disappearance, that point at which the notes stopped, or should have stopped. But trying to contain it all, to filter and find a coherent meaning, is beyond me.

I think that's why I'm still writing this – it does seem to help. Writing for myself, alone. As, I guess, he was too.

Light is confusing me again. It feels brighter and sharper here than anywhere else I've been. It feels open in the way that city lights are closed: there they focus and burn, cutting pools of safety into the night, or drawing colours on walls and pavements, windows and roads. Here the light is a single thing. A complete flood, filling every gap.

And when the light goes, the darkness is total in a way a city can never imagine. City darkness is just different light. Mountain darkness is pure, thick ink. It is deeper than colour, but also absent. Both a black hole and a flat wall you cannot pass, permanently inches from your face.

The two do not deserve the same word. It doesn't work hard enough for what it means out here, how it really feels.

City darkness can be fun, exciting, exhilarating, like when we first met, back then. That was a city, at night, the darkness of a small bar. A jazz club, smoking inside when that was still allowed, everyone trying just a little too hard. Carefully poised to look like they didn't care, as if they were truly absorbed in the music, not scouring the room for lust and opportunity. She glowed, in that darkness, and we shyly met. She was waiting for friends, friends who were late. From their lateness we became possible, we grew.

And we ran through the streets that night, laughing at the moon, faces slapped red from the cold, warmed inside by wine, by the promise of something. Something that came to be and is now lost. That was another kind of darkness, before this.

The darkness out here still scares me. It has been a few weeks of heading out into the mountains and deeper into the forest, but in daylight only. The night is too much.

5.15pm. Dark now. Inside.

That one is definitely from earlier in his stay and, I think, the longer pieces about a devil are more recent, but I might be wrong. The times and weather observations give faint clues, but never enough. Nothing connects.

I've been wondering about trying to place them all in some sort of order, spread them back out across the stone floor again, but there is just too much to work with. I am trying to rearrange droplets in the ocean.

There are, however, individual pages that stand out. They mean more than the others. Sometimes it's the extremity of his emotions, the loss of control, and other times it's a feeling that one particular piece of paper throws something else into relief. A flash of light in the darkness.

I returned to the hotel today, feeling drawn, compelled. Something is there – is she? This is our place, after all, these glens and these slopes.

The stark white paint had faded, peeled, cracked, blackened by damp and mould at its edges. The trees around it, once cut down to open up the views, are now growing back, reclaiming this space for the forest. Hiding it, enclosing it.

We came here, so long ago, but couldn't get near to it. To its wealth and noise, its lights burning their way into the wilderness. Taking what was not there to be taken.

I shrank away from that red light, that CCTV camera, real or not, and approached the hotel from behind.

I could feel it. There is something there.

6.43pm. Stormy.

The notes should have stopped when he left here, moved on to wherever he is now. The notes did stop, surely stopped.

I hear his words over and over.

Don't run. Don't pack. Don't hide the pages.

I have brought them together, those impossible notes, piled on the cottage table. It is brighter today, sunlight pooling on the uneven grey floor. Each page feels like a surprise from nowhere. They are all too close, from someone watching who cannot be watching.

He is not here and could not have done this. He is not here and would not have done this.

And yet I want more. I want to be shocked again, as nothing else could bring hope. Nothing else could bring him back.

But what if they don't attach to each other, to now, to me? What if they weren't echoes, responses, part of a conversation between my thoughts and his paper furies?

What if, sadly, they speak to nothing but his continued disintegration? If he could imagine a devil looming over that hollow then of course he could imagine far simpler, far more ordinary things. His pages are not impossible, not arriving from somewhere unexplained. They are just painful beyond words, beyond any words I have.

I was confused, in my own grief, as he was in his. I found those notes in a cloud of shock, understandably shocked, read them and felt I hadn't read them, read them and thought them new, spirited from nowhere. I spoke to myself through his words, collected pieces that don't fit. My brain was making connections that don't exist, surely it was.

All there is is grief and forest and loneliness. Memories of parents, of arguing in sorrow, of shouting, then nothing.

There is nothing left to explain.

There is so much I have seen and so much still to see.

I must keep going, keep going towards her.

Step by step by step.

7.29am. Warming.

Another day. I woke early in my new, temporary home, ate quickly, grabbed water and food to take with me, and hurried back to the cottage. There is sanctuary in the little house I'm staying in, with its unseen neighbours and warm bed, the only warm place I have found here so far. But it doesn't feel like security I deserve, or that I can be drawn into just yet. Domestic comfort is its own devil.

Outside was dark, night still hanging over, thick clouds shuffling across the sky, promising rain. Each morning is the same, performing a private ritual. Out, drive, follow the edge of the looming loch, the twisting roads that hang precariously over the silver water, then eventually turn off the road and into the forest, and keep going and going until the cottage appears.

Take the ice-cold padlock that rattles as it moves, unlock, and take a deep breath.

There is a tiny moment of sheer panic every time I enter. I have to steel myself for it, holding on to the door, pausing for a moment and then walking in suddenly. As if I can surprise away whatever I fear is inside.

Each time I expect to see something changed: another note, a rearranged pile of papers that will shake me to my bones once again, even though that never was, that never could have been.

But nothing. Every morning, nothing.

This morning was the same.

NOTES

WHAT ARE THESE NOTES

PAPER FRIENDS

PAPER PROTECTION

NO HELP

NO HELP WILL COME

HIDDEN NOW

GONE

Noon

1.

This is my favourite time of day. I've climbed above the tree line, where it becomes too rough, too precarious for anything tall to grow. A curved edge that swoops from mountain to mountain, marking the end of shelter, the beginning of exposure and real struggle.

In trying to find meaning in the notes themselves, it feels I have been missing something. Looking the wrong way. I need to investigate both the words and the mountains. Neither means anything without the other.

But I know I will never get through every page, or be able to match each to its place and time, its light and weather. I need a way of bringing the words and the world closer together, to see more of what Dad saw.

I'm starting by trying to find some of the places where he may have stopped, or even written, though it seems that almost all the writing took place back at the cottage. It was a capturing, or purging, of what had come before, after some sort of crazed attempt to find my dead

Mum, whose body has long since turned to ash hundreds of miles away. The pages show no signs of creasing from being carried in a backpack, or any damage from rain. The paper is pristine, even though the words are not.

The sun has nearly risen now, and the morning mist I saw driving in has been burnt away. The shadows of early morning light have shortened as the sun stretches overhead, becoming stubby, nearly non-existent, waiting until they can return.

Noon in the mountains carries so many family memories of quiet pausing, eating and replenishing. On a good day this would be at the top, having reached a peak, drinking in the views, the whole world below and nothing left above. No further to go.

On a bad day, however, noon has a different weight. I have repeatedly felt the discomfort of calculating the time to the peak, the time to sunset, the balance of safety and success. Holding back the animal within you that wants to continue, to push on regardless.

In those moments, Mum and Dad were always far calmer than me. That desperation to summit, to keep on and keep on, just didn't seem to touch them. Together they were complete. Moving together as one was enough. It wasn't enough for me, and it still isn't.

I turn away and keep climbing. I keep searching.

This isn't working. The tests, the experiments aren't working. Too sloppy, too vague, too many moving parts to see what is really going on.

64

I must focus, refine, improve. I must change, and change quickly.

There is not enough time.

6.03am. Dark.

The testing I find very surprising. Dad was structured, but he was certainly not a scientist or engineer. He worked as an administrator, for the government long ago, and later for councils and a university or two. A professional purveyor of order, someone who could be trusted to find meaning in complexity. He found clarity, often for others who could not.

Which is perhaps why the experiments feel childish and amateur, and why they feel so painful. He is reaching for a method, a way of testing, of proving or disproving before moving on. But it is chaos and his emotions are wild, like a hunted animal.

I will improve. Must improve. Must find a way to learn, to step forward and forward.

She is here and where am I? Nowhere, despite travelling, climbing, hiking, falling.

Time to change how I am looking. I am looking for her and have seen nothing.

No more.

8.23am. Dawning.

I am watching the world below as if I am not part of it, something held behind glass, a perfect curiosity I can never touch. I want to sleep, to sink into silence, but I also want to push on. I want to feel it hurting.

Everything inside me is turmoil and will not ease, so I am trying to scour it out, scratch away my feelings from the inside. Burn everything by running straight up a mountain until I collapse, until it ends.

Earlier this morning I attacked the slope too fiercely, too quickly. I brought too much to it – too much hope and expectation, too much to carry. I wanted to find him now, or to punish myself if I failed again.

So far I have found nothing. It might have to be enough that I'm moving, searching, not static and stuck. For now.

This place should be perfect and calm, it should be adventuring, escaping from office and mortgage, from the flood of perfect online lives, carved and crafted, marked by insecurity at their edges. Shiny and frayed. But there is just me, an empty wilderness, and a fury of paper notes that shift and move as much as the branches high above.

And a fox. A single, silent creature gliding from behind a huge rock, tracing invisible lines, ready for danger. Poised, sprung, an explosion waiting to happen.

It looks straight at me, experiencing the world in ways I can't even imagine, navigating through layers of scent, distant sounds, and threats. It stares. I am still, holding my breath closely, trying to keep from any movement, any suggestion that I want this to end.

It is sheer beauty. Lithe, fierce, pure independence. It disappears into the trees.

Testing, always testing. I need to find some sort of structure, a way of looking closely, of ruling in or ruling out.

I need to turn the mountain into a grid, a series of boxes that can be tracked, searched, scrutinised one by one.

To move slowly, methodically, from one to the next.

But everything changes. How many times must I look?

9.17am. Some light, some cloud.

My mind feels busy sometimes, a wind tearing through me, even as I steadily walk back to the cottage, head pounding from hours of overexertion. Busy with ideas coming all at once, repeating and repeating, drawing circles. Noisy circles. Can a circle get louder as it spins, as it turns in on itself?

I don't know. I'm trying to place this into words, to find some way of securing the thought to the page. Sometimes this works, but often it doesn't. If it didn't hurt so much, this would be fascinating, that my words are never really mine, that they feel constantly on loan from someone else. Possibly someone I don't know, don't like, or who doesn't like me.

For a long time I have been angry, confused that I can be separated from myself by language, that I can never put down what I am thinking with any clarity or precision.

I watch myself thinking and walking, distracted, my foot nearly caught by a sharp rock jutting out of the ground. Lost in my own thoughts, far away from wherever I am.

What am I looking for? He is gone, surely gone, and will not be found. I touch the roughness of the tree bark as I pass, listen to the wind, and spot birds flitting in the branches.

Back near the cottage I see a faded white mark on a tree trunk that has fallen, a small cross that has almost been washed away by the rain. An echo of forestry management perhaps, of someone long gone.

So far everything has been wasted. The time, the effort, all of these words. All pointless, pulled the wrong way, diverted. I have lost every moment, every decision, every opportunity to take a step closer to finding her. I am right here, but she is further away than she has ever been.

Today I start again. I must recognise the Devil's voice, its quiet torment, its call to complacency and laziness.

I am starting from a foul realisation: everything I enjoy is poison, confusion, and smokescreen. I enjoy climbing, running, exploring the mountains, so I push to climb, run, and explore, as we did together. The long days of dried sweat crusting on neck and forehead, the comfortable glide into a rhythm of step, step, follow, step, step, look.

I am here, searching, pleading, in despair, but still I enjoy the morning sun, cresting a peak, watching the light fade from another day. And I am wrong to.

Everything is irrelevant, but her. Everything I enjoy must be cast away, blocked out.

The Devil knows this. It has her. It is blinding me with beauty, gently pulling my attention away without me ever noticing.

I must find a way to surprise, to no longer be myself. I need to look at the world as someone else, detach and assess. Today I start again.

10.20am. Bright.

I am back at the cottage now, out of breath, in some pain from the recklessness of the morning. I need to drink water, to eat, to recover, to give my body a chance to catch up with me. Sweat is in my eyes and stinging now. I can taste it when I drink too, so I step outside to wash in the river. I am following in his footsteps.

It is fast, bringing water down from the mountains, rain and snow-melt passing through at speed. I stand on the muddy bank and plunge my head under, shocked by the brutally low temperature but invigor-ated too. I scrub at my face and hair with my hands, feeling the salt dissolve and disappear.

Once clean, I walk slowly back inside to tidy up the pages I've brought out of the boxes, to try and impose my own order, to bring my understanding to everything that has happened. I am trying to shape this space into something that is mine, that is safe, where I can rest.

The tidying takes me back to when we were settling into our new house, that one and only time. It was a mid-terrace with a narrow garden, fenced in on both sides. I remember gazing at the fading wallpaper that needed to be scraped off, and the beautiful old fireplace, framed in shining blue tiles.

The flat we'd left was also over two levels, but there was one more step in the new house, one more movement to complete the descent. And for years afterwards my body would expect the ground to hold me too early, only to fall for a moment, shocked that the floor wasn't where it should be. At night this was particularly startling, a heart-racing moment of unwanted adrenaline. Even returning later as an adult, I would still have the same awful shock over and over again.

Words are missing steps, or extra steps. They are never where you need them to be, never behaving as they should. They should connect and console us. They should release the pressure inside. But they don't.

I jump at a terrible noise outside, a screaming, flapping burst. A bird frightened, caught, dead? I've been in my own little world, not noticing the darkness crashing in again. I look out and can see nothing, can hear nothing.

Everything is fine, it must be fine, but I need to get away now. Lock the cottage, into the car, lights on, and try to breathe through the long journey out of the forest.

Try not to look too hard at the shadows waving in my rear-view mirror.

SEE YOU NOW

BUT YOU DO NOT SEE

WAITING

WATCHING

PATIENT

2.

It's a new day, back to the mountains, this time taking some words with me. It is grey and clouded, but dry for now.

I felt uncomfortable at the cottage earlier, stifled inside those thick stone walls. Every noise dragged me to a window or to the threshold, to look, to check. Feeling hunted again. I had to get out, to climb my way free.

Occasionally sunlight bursts through overhead, then is quickly smothered. I have brought a small notepad which fits easily into my coat pocket. In it are the brief notes I've been taking, copying out his words, trying to frame them, to edit and tease some clarity from his dense, fogged pages.

> It was too dark out. I'd been watching the sky earlier, the colours changing places with each other, the light cutting sharp through the clouds. The crimson and navy waves, before the cold night falls.

Darkness was always something Dad struggled with and tried to dismiss. He talked once of an early memory of his, spending a holiday with distant relatives, an old farmhouse with strong, strange smells, another world from the plain, neat suburbia of his childhood. Red-brick terrace, lawn, and tarmac swapped for manure, wellies, and rats darting between cavernous barns. I wasn't clear if his parents were staying there, or if he was alone. I wasn't clear if he could remember either.

He was cold and vacant recalling all of this, and he was only sharing because I'd been scared of something too. What it was, I can no longer remember. He was trying to show me that fear is fine, it is natural, something that can be tamed, handled, overcome. But he utterly failed in this, drawing out a memory too strong, too violent to offer any comfort. I still don't quite understand why he went there, or whether he needed to tell the story more than I needed to hear it.

A young relative, a cousin several times removed, offered to show him around the farm, to have an adventure in the barns. It was a thrill, this freedom to roam and explore, to play and stray, quite unlike the strict limits he was set at home. As the sun was falling, the heat coming out of the day, they kept walking the fields, climbing fences, throwing stones, laughing. Simple and easy.

Then to the lower barns, at the bottom of the fields, just out of sight from the main house. When he described that stench of animal dung, the foul intensity of it, and the darkness inside, his voice changed, the softness sharpening to a sneer.

Dad climbed a ladder, and then felt a push. A shove into a pile of dried hay, tiny scratches and spikes lodged in his hair, and a fading laugh as the cousin sped back down the rungs, across the barn, and

73

dragged the heavy doors shut. Metal wheels scraping and screeching in their rusting groove. And darkness.

Darkness, heat, and pure disorientation.

Night-time here is too dark for words. It is nothing.

He told me that story with a blankness on his face, as if it had happened to someone else, or was a scene from a film he saw many years ago. One where he'd forgotten most of the details, the story and actors, but one violent sequence stayed with him. He had tried to find the ladder back down to the barn's floor, from where it should have been easy to find a wall, and trace around the huge dark rectangle until he found the way out. The cousin always insisted it was just a joke, just a game, pleading through his own hot tears.

Dad fell. He fell from the upper level, or loft, or wherever it was he had been pushed. He landed on cold, hard concrete, and wasn't found for some time. He lay in the darkness, breathing in the manure, pain coursing through his body. A broken ankle, several shattered fingers, a lot of blood lost. Some quiet talk of compound fractures, of bones snapped and forced through skin. Whispers of panic, blue lights, ambulance, hospital, brightness fading in and out. He was as pale as snow when he told that part.

He always called that cousin a devil.

Dark nights and bright mornings. Each day is a blessing. A blessing that fades.

There's a spot beyond the forest, just before the slope really kicks up, where a large rock rests. He seems to have sat there a lot, both on the

74

way up and the way down the mountain, either pausing before a major exertion or gently stopping after.

> *The beauty from the peaks is too obvious. It is totally overpowering. From lower down you can see so much more, the texture and rhythm of trees, physical memories of human planting and nature's drift. Something you can feel attached to. Something that tells you more about being a small, silent human, rather than tricking you into a brief delusion of being a god, sitting far above a world that cannot touch you, until it does.*

Sometimes his notes help, sometimes they don't. There is always some darkness, even at the brightest moment of the day.

BRIGHT BRIGHT

LOOK LOOK

DARK DARK

DROWN

I sit on the large rock, trying to get closer to him by sharing his space, touching the rough stone, fingernails scratching over lichen, its muted greens and greys, working it loose, thinking of barnacles and waves, thinking of how life persists in the most wonderful, strange ways.

> *Today I tried to run the edge of the forest as far as I could, to follow its line, to understand why it stops and why it starts, to look for gaps. To look for her.*

There is so much that I still don't understand. I am watching the trees in the wind, hearing the birds hidden in the branches, uncertain which bird is calling and why. Thinking about this too hard takes something away. It is a pure discomfort. Mum would have known.

That certainty has gone, that reassuring ability to look to another to resolve some restlessness in yourself, to calm and compose.

There is so much here, and so little.

He is here and not here. I hear his voice in every moment, and have even found myself turning, spinning around in the woods, expecting him to be standing there. To be found.

He isn't here.

Is he?

LOOK

LOOK THE WRONG WAY

THE ONE WAY

AWAY

AWAY

AWAY

I am delaying the trip back down, trying to ignore and contain my discomfort. And there, on the horizon, a walker. I haven't seen anyone here for so long. This part of the forest is beyond remote. It is far away from the guidebook recommendations, with no easy access to the road or any of the better-known summits, and not even accidentally on the route between somewhere and somewhere else.

To see a walker here is rare, extremely rare. So far I've not seen anyone inside the forest as it is too dense, too dark, and have only spotted a handful of people up on the mountains. People at distance, always at distance.

This is somewhere to be lost and little more. But I watch as the small figure leans into the slope with purpose, hands on knees, working hard against the ground. Pausing occasionally for breath. I can almost see their joy from here. I can feel it.

Dad has a neon red jacket like that, had a neon red jacket like that. Bright and unnatural in the wilderness. To be seen in snow, to be seen in darkness. Bright enough to be found, to be saved when lost. I think of helicopter searches, ravines and worse, and force the thought away. I think of another walker spotting a flash of fabric hidden, resting, where gravity has ended, and force the thought away.

He had a neon red jacket like that. Actually, he took that jacket when he went, when he ran after the funeral. After my burning words. He took the most garish jacket he owned, the most luminous item of clothing he probably ever bought, to disappear in. I nearly laugh at this horrendous clash.

But that's not it: he wasn't trying to disappear, even if that is what happened. His focus was on something else entirely. On rescuing.

The walker is nearing a steeper slope and slips out of view, behind a rocky outcrop, then comes back. Again, hands on knees, looking down then up, tracking the loose ground and the horizon, bringing the two closer together.

I am restless, flinching. Could it be? It couldn't be.

He is dead. Surely he is dead. He has to be. The notes, those awful notes, that they don't make sense, can't make sense. That I've been looking away, deliberately and mercilessly, from the growing certainty of his death.

No, not that. Looking away, but reluctantly, sadly, trying to protect myself from the threat of reality, trying to find shelter in structure, to find safety and sanity where there are none. Trying to avoid the hollow, trying to avoid the truth.

Could it be?

I'm up now. It can't be, but I'll move over that way regardless. How far? Maybe a mile or so, over some really rough terrain. How long? Fifteen minutes of hard walking? Ten at a run, if it's smooth enough to run? Maybe, but probably not. I don't want to stumble and trip, to be picking grit from bloodied hands as he continues to move further and further away.

But where will he be then? Not where he is now, but another ten or fifteen minutes further up. Thinking of triangles and school maths puzzles, connecting time and movement and direction. Where will he be in one of my miles? Where will we meet?

The straight line isn't the safest route. I need to climb a little higher, to find a smoother edge to trace across, at least the suggestion of a path, a line followed by wild animals, padding across the mountainside. My hands on my own knees now, looking up, stones grinding under my feet. Stepping up and sliding down, a sensation I took such joy in when I was younger now just slowing me, building a frustration, an anger and impatience.

It is that neon red jacket. It really is. But his? Him? Don't get too far ahead of yourself, just move, keep moving. This isn't crazy, I'm simply taking a walk. A fevered walk, perhaps, but a walk. Just taking a walk, although I am running now. The ground has levelled off, softened slightly, and I can move faster. Less stony, less severe, though I'm still on a sharp slope. There is a long way to fall.

Remember your footsteps beneath you. Look up and look down. Don't get lost in the horizon, only to let him suddenly drift and disappear.

Properly running now. What do I say? What do I do? How do you approach your vanished father on a deserted mountain? How do you approach your dead dad as he takes a walk?

Getting closer now, maybe five minutes to go until we meet. The slope has shifted, as it always does, morphing as you climb, revealing more peaks behind, further slopes and rises, hollows and outcrops. His route has changed, and there's a sheer rock face ahead that was hidden from view just a few minutes ago. I can't see him now. To follow around, to climb? I've climbed rocks like that before, just a few metres, but no, no, no. I can feel the momentum now, can feel it building in my head. Recognise it, know it, don't listen to it.

I run past the rising cliff, looking away from it. Could climb it, don't climb it. Have climbed far higher, far worse, far trickier. Don't climb it. Brain fogging now, breath not helping, moving on and on. Where is he? Who is he?

Something has changed. I'm past the rocky face, but the land has shifted again. Nothing is where it was. The slope has rippled, the mountain has taken a breath and turned.

Keep moving, keep moving. That neon red jacket, it is still here, somewhere here. Think of all those peaks that disappear without disappearing. That may be lost from your limited view, your limited imagination, but are still there, waiting far, far above.

But this is different, it is surely different. Again with the breath, find the breath, feeling the panic as it catches, as it turns from gas to solid. As it turns to bone. Moving helps, always helps. Keep moving up.

Up and up. There is more here, more that I can see. Hear? Nothing but the wind's impatience. It is tired of me now, wants me away. Up and up.

Above the rock face now, I feel the ground shifting again, seeing the land as it moves, as it is made. I make more of it with each step. Where am I in this? Where is he?

Is he trying to escape again? I hadn't even thought that before. He is hiding and has been found. He is running, surely he is running from me. I am trying to climb the slope, feeling the slick mud and rock beneath. Keep going, keep going up.

Past and past, moving up, around a ridge. And there, a face. A neon red jacket and a face. A sudden, surprised, smiling face.

The wrong face.

Greying, older, happy to see a fellow hiker despite not knowing me. This stranger is kind and welcoming while I am distant and distraught, broken into pieces all over again.

LOOKING

LOOKING

SEEING

FALLING

What do you do when everything stops? How do you respond, react? How do you cope? How do you step forward, find a way to stay alive?

A neon red jacket and a face. A him, but not him. Not his age, but near enough his build. That same jacket, but not him.

Is he here?

Is he still here?

I am falling, all over again.

I am falling and nothing can stop me.

WATCHING

WAITING

HIDING

I am settling a little now, beginning to recover. How could I explain to someone what is happening in my head, why I am here? How could I explain my pleading eyes and everything that lies behind them?

There is a startle, for him, and a vacuum for me. My first conversation with anyone in weeks. I have nothing to give, but it doesn't seem to matter. Some breathless pleasantries, light words on weather and mountains and fine days and I hear it'll turn again soon. Wind and rain coming, snow will follow soon after.

A sense of him wanting to stay here, but knowing he needs to leave before the winter comes in hard, before the roads are closed at the snow gates, the orange metal barriers that sit and threaten all year round. A sense of him choosing to go back home. He leaves with a parting smile, as open as sunshine.

Then I turn to go back, back down towards the cottage, but slower this time.

I feel light, dizzy, as if the mountain is moving beneath me, trying to throw me off my feet. I am not welcome here.

EDGES

THERE ARE EDGES YOU SEE

AND EDGES YOU DO NOT

He was there, for a moment, a brief moment of self-deception. I filled up with words to say, with love and anger, with guilt and remorse, with questions. How, why? And why here? Why would she be here, if she was alive, if she was trapped, whatever that could mean?

I know that this was a place for them, the dot on their old map, but surely somewhere safely in the past. Not a place to run to from the funeral, from my shouting, my love and anger and despair. My heated words for the world, words that were never for him but were pointed at him. That were felt by him.

I am still full of questions that never end. I need to let them go, but do not know how, do not know where. I went looking for where he wrote, found something else, then instantly lost it.

I need to start but have no idea what starting is.

YOU LOOK LIKE YOU WOULD BURN

BURN INTO NOTHING

QUIET AND ALONE

PART OF THE FOREST

PART OF THE MOUNTAIN

ASH AND ROCK AND WIND AND RAIN

3.

The meeting with the lone walker yesterday hurt and has left me feeling embarrassed and ashamed. That I let go, believed, trusted. That I ran away with myself so quickly. That I found, for a moment, then lost all over again. An emptiness that grows and grows.

Another memory of loneliness rushes back, late in university, the final year, the chase towards an ending. Classes started to fade away, structure slowly dissolved, while all around was the most tremendous pressure to succeed. To make something of yourself, to set a course for the rest of your life. To confirm a choice made long ago, by circumstance or family expectation.

It was terrifying. By that point I was living alone, and with a gap of weeks and months to a few brief exams that would judge my value, at least as I saw it then.

HAVE FOUND THESE SMALL SPACES NOW TOO

From the Christmas of that year onward, time slowed and stretched. I felt uncomfortable in every moment, in every breath. A noise inside me growing and growing. I would go to lectures, methodically arriving three minutes after they started and leaving three minutes before they ended, to avoid having to speak to anyone. I sat in a corner by the door for just long enough to collect the information, then took it away, back to my den. I couldn't bring myself to attend any smaller group sessions, and soon stopped giving any reasons.

It was dark. I would see people I knew, some I knew well, some I liked very much, but there were no words. No words that could bridge the gap between us. My eyes would beg people for help, but I imagine all they saw was a stare. To them it must have been confusing, or simply dismissed as being rude. To me it was cold agony, day and night.

Dad talks somewhere of dark nights and bright mornings. Of how neither are necessarily good or bad. Brightness can be glory, joy, warmth, and comfort. It can also be blinding, disorientating, painful. The bright morning may not be full of joy, it may need to be hidden from.

I felt this, in those final months at university, waking to a lurking, invisible pain every day.

LISTEN LISTEN

QUIET NOW

It was January, a hard winter, heavy with solitude and silence. This was before the internet came with us everywhere, in our pockets and bags, before its structured isolation bled into every part of our lives.

I hid from everything. Going for supplies couldn't be avoided but it could happen late, after the risk had faded of stumbling upon friend-liness and warmth from anyone I knew. Worst of all was when I was spotted by those who missed me, had been delighted by an earlier me, another me, and wanted to share in something I couldn't.

I had months to go, and a simple rage to finish at university. To survive that long, and to see what would happen next. To think any further was to play with impossibilities, was to risk opening a gap that was too wide to close.

I took small steps. Get up, wash, eat, work two hours, break, work two hours, eat, work two hours, break, work two hours, run, wash, eat, work two hours, sleep. And again and again and again, every day.

What sticks with me most vividly was the constant feeling of grinding. Not fierce or severe, just something rubbing all the time. Sometimes soft and quiet, distant and humming, sometimes loud and over-whelming. Always, always grinding. I could never quite understand if I was wearing something away, being worn away myself, or even craft-ing something useful or beautiful. I am still not sure.

YOUR WORDS

YOUR DARKNESS

LISTEN

Those were hard days. I learnt everything, I did the exams, there were grades and numbers and celebrations all around me. Paper-prepared for the world. It all felt like someone else's achievement.

I could feel and hear this thing happening to me, or me happening to it, for four or five months. Counting down the minutes to two hours, then break. Counting down, then eat. Counting down, then break. Counting down, then run, eat, wash. Counting down, then sleep. Then start again.

The darkest thoughts came then. Big shapeless clouds that block out the light until you no longer realise you are sitting in shadow. It is not that you are in the dark, but that everything is dark. It becomes a solid mass, a single tone sounding out evenly and endlessly. All is smooth and clear, tasteless and textureless.

YES

LISTEN LISTEN

MORE MORE YOU

Everything seems clear, but you can't see clearly. You can't see far at all. All there is is step, step, step. To remember that this has happened before, that the only rule is to never stop moving. To stop is to slip into silence, to breathe in that shapeless cloud, to become part of it. To believe it.

87

That's the other rule: don't believe it. What you can see now is not all there is. Much is hidden, and to find it you must move and move and never, ever stop moving.

NO

THIS IS COMFORT

SLOW STOP

REST STOP

I ran every night through those months, the exact same route. From my small, dull student flat to a city park, barely five minutes away. Each time it felt as if I had been holding my breath for twenty-four hours, and that I had a few precious moments to collect enough air to last the next day. Enough coldness and pain, enough sweat and grimace, enough speed to remember that everything is movement and I am never stopped. Just paused, ready and twitching to go again.

And as the weeks passed I became fitter and fitter. Not competitive or anything close to an athlete, but more than I was before. Not different, but more me and more of me. Many people don't understand this, both those who run and those who don't. That I am not racing anyone, and if I was I would never be racing anyone but myself. I am in motion, and there is nothing else in the world.

Step, step, step. Steps cannot be alone.

NO

MORE NEEDED

MORE YOU

AND MORE THIS

MORE DARK

MORE DARKNESS

MORE

Those evening runs were precious and life-giving, even though they were short. Maybe twenty or twenty-five minutes at the most, not the hours you can spend walking, pausing, and watching out here.

They were critical minutes, though, despite the incessant low hum of discontent. That feeling of permanently choking on ice would soften and even, sometimes, stop. Stopping as I moved faster, as the wind pushed back against me, as my muscles tensed and sang, as my feet tapped, tapped, tapped. It felt so natural and right, it made everything else seem irrational and pointless.

At its best running can make a world of worries and pain disappear. Those feelings of frustration and worthlessness fade into a blank non-existence. But in those months nothing was at its best. Back then the running was simple survival.

Breathing in enough to be given life, softening the pain a little, finding some colour in all the grinding grey. Remembering that something else was possible, that it could change. That was all I could hold on to, never daring to consider that it actually would change. That I would.

Back then, I just wanted some quiet.

Silence was enough. Surviving was enough.

They will have to be enough again.

4.

This is day one. Or maybe day zero. A new start, where nothing is known and everything is to be mistrusted. The beautiful calm, the warming of the winter sun, geese drawing lines through the sky. All are distraction, none are relevant.

I am starting with the forest, the trees around the cottage. I will inspect and mark every tree, climbing them where I can, noting how they look, so I can see how they change over time. To see if anything is shifting around me, crucial details lost because the picture is too big to look at.

The mountains are majestic, so for now they are to be ignored too. They will come later.

6.19pm. Raining.

Each night I return to my rented house, tired, strained, mind still racing despite my body being still. This house is everything the cottage is not, and has everything it doesn't. A fridge, a cooker, a toilet, a bath.

More than one room. In the evening I turn on the heating, lie under a rough blue blanket on an old sofa now worn smooth. Every time I wonder what comes next.

Yesterday I found more of the marks on nearby trees, all pretty close to the cottage but rain-washed and barely visible now. I now realise he made these, but why he did still feels unclear. He had another moment of starting again, something else we share. The marks are all in white chalk, either circles or crosses. I have no idea what they mean, if they mean anything at all.

On the big rock by the forest's edge I also saw what appears to be a small, neat circle worn into the lichen. Any chalk had been completely washed away, as it is exposed to all weather, but there still seemed to be a shape. I couldn't tell if it was there, or if I just wanted it to be.

Today I will look for more of the chalk markings, and start to sketch my own maps, to find any patterns, any connections between them. Inside the forest they have been sheltered from the rain and can be seen reasonably clearly, at least up close. Beyond there may have been many, many more, but they will all be washed away by now.

I spent the whole day stepping, inspecting, marking, noting, moving on. Exposed roots, rot, dead mice, branches torn off in storms.

Bark with serrated edges, occasional tiny holes and ruts in the ground, echoes of burrowing, but nothing that told me anything useful.

And tomorrow I will repeat and retrace. I will note changes. I will challenge everything I see, every time.

8.31pm. Wind pushing through.

The sun is straight above, glaring down. I am walking past the forest's perimeter, feeling both the midday heat and the chill of a late autumn day. A push and pull of just too warm and just too cool, waves that never settle, never still. Everything looks immaculate, picture-perfect, but to be here is something else. There are tensions I can feel but can't see.

I am restless, itching to move, impatient with everything. I want none of this to be happening, but want it to happen all at once. To burn through grief in one go. To end it.

The changes here are strong and subtle, sometimes swift, sometimes glacial. However she is trapped, however it is hiding her is behind something small, dull, and secret.

The way in isn't big or grand, there is no cave with a tunnel lurking deep within, waiting to be stumbled on at the right time on the right day. There is no solstice waiting to illuminate everything.

The Devil is hiding in front of me. I have seen everything and overlooked it. I know that now.

4.43pm. Cold and cooling.

Momentum is a word that crops up often in his pages, and it's something I've been thinking about a lot recently. Both how momentum can be confidence and strength, but also risk and recklessness. How important it is to balance gathering speed with the fear of not being able to stop.

I have lost all momentum. There is nothing left. I need to start moving again, but starting is always the hardest. Once up and out the door, into the light, everything eases.

I have felt momentum, pushing me through life, and the cruel dead stop when it is lost. In these woods and on the slopes it can be easy to find, particularly coming downhill, pulled by gravity, adrenaline, and joyful acceleration. I feel it now, finding these chalk marks, being led by them, starting to plot their positions and where they point to, where they lead.

But it often stops. It was in mountains like these I had the worst injury of my life, just as the confidence tipped too far, the split-second after thinking all is perfect and well, that the movement will never stop.

I was not long out of university, having graduated with some distinction. A summer of other people celebrating, friendships already burnt out, being caught between everything before and everything yet to come. I needed to start again.

And I chose to start again up in the mountains. Back to the Lake District, retracing my childhood footsteps, looking for familiarity as I felt nothing but difference. I felt close to tears for most of that summer, not in darkness or even sad as such. Just too much emotion, too much energy with nowhere to go.

At the start I was angry. Aimless anger that took weeks to control. Nothing that could be explained or rationalised, but a rawness that stayed and waited. Patient, furious rage that wanted an end to everything. It still comes back occasionally, but I know it now.

So I ran. I ran every day for weeks, living alone, but making passing connections to other adventurers drawn to escape. There was a quiet acceleration, almost imperceptible but real and solid and hard. It was beautiful to become something new, to see my body change ever so slightly, to feel as if the hills were flattening, slopes less steep, oxygen coursing through me.

And those runs, once or twice a day, showed me a different side of myself. I loved to feel free. Each day I would climb up a steep slope, usually slowly, lost in thought or lost with no thought, just for a few gleeful moments of coming back down again.

The descents were total silence. The cacophony of doubt and fury muted for brief seconds. It was all about edges, of balancing control and deliberately letting go. Deciding, at the start, that everything would be too quick, that to even think would be to risk falling, to risk death.

> I felt out of control today. It has been raining and the scree is sliding, rough but frictionless. Rocky sheets of ice.

And in motion you stop. You are moving far quicker than you ever could on flat ground. You are leaping over boulders and streams, your brain spotting and guessing and moving your foot placement mid-air, pivoting your ankle at the last chance, twisting away from a stone that looks loose, hopping, picking up your knee so you land past a shining tree root, remembering somewhere deep inside that wet roots are the most lethal surface of all, choosing to slide in mud while you process what can come next, then picking between murky water and a soft grassy edge, whichever is less likely to turn you, twist you, and break you. Inside all of that there is no space for anything else. It is all pure, beautiful nothing.

Until it stops. Until you think about it, let yourself believe that you can do this, or even more stupidly take the tiniest fraction of a second to wonder how good this must look, if anyone else was here watching, deep in this empty wilderness. Wouldn't this make a great photograph?

In that moment the mountain will punish you, quickly and mercilessly, in one of a thousand ways.

My mistake was to simply think how much I was enjoying myself. That killed the rhythm, pushed the swaying balance too far one way, and by a centimetre or two I missed a flat landing. The side of my heel caught on a rock, I stumbled, twisted away, then couldn't turn inwards with the path. The mountain had its own movement, which mine had been close enough to, overlapping, steering in and out, but within a safe margin. Then the edge comes, you stray, you fall.

It happens before you know it. You are caught watching yourself in a mirror, looking back on moments before, observing someone else's ridiculous smile and misplaced confidence. Then gravity pulls fast and hard, flesh dragged over rocks, blood streaked over frayed and ripped sports clothing.

Your body's tumbling slows, friction building its own momentum, pushing back as you push forward. Forces crashing into each other, with weak bones and body caught in the middle, all of your life and energy drained.

Your breathing is different, still quick but unreliable and gasping, not strong and deep as before. Eyes closed and pain flashing, a lag from now to now, nerves sending signals that can't be understood right away.

> *I am more scared of these mountains than ever. When we were here together it was all a simple challenge, a balance of effort and reward. Now I understand that effort is fickle and unreliable. We never know what the challenge really is, how deep it goes.*

I went over the edge of the path, maybe halfway down from the peak. At that height the trails are narrow, as much routes for water streaming down as for people climbing up, far above the comfortable paths near the bottom, where families and dogs and casual Sunday walkers have cut safety and familiarity into the hillsides over years and years and years.

Pain has texture and heat and sound. It's not just a signal, an alert to be noted and replied to. This pain was multiple, deep and bassy, shrill and sharp, with a burning centre and cold edges. Soft and lulling, dull, but spiked and cutting. Ice can still burn, I thought, before everything went silent.

I came to and thought of Mum and Dad, of being found and held and cared for, knowing that could not and would not happen. It was August and the mountains were busy, but I had left early and the weather was poor. It could be hours until anyone chanced on this same route, or came close enough to hear my weak cries. I thought of Dad, the cousin, the barn. He was pushed. I pushed myself.

For hours I watched the sun stretch across the sky. Clouds gathering, merging, shifting and distorting. I heard bird cries but little else. I had run without a phone or whistle, further stupidities that were to be punished. Then a sudden rush of being found, a worried face, an emergency call, mountain rescue, and overwhelming guilt. Guilt at my weakness and need, guilt at being seen when all I'd come to the mountains for was to disappear.

There was some panic, a hospital stay, and then a long, long recovery to moving properly again. Pain and prodding, and endless, mindless physio exercises. But as I'd done before and have done since, in many less dramatic situations, I kept going. Being beaten by the mountain doesn't make you want to stop. It makes you want to go back and do it right. The fire burns brighter.

LISTEN

QUIET VOICE

DEEP INSIDE

HUNTING YOU

How many other chalk shapes have washed away and been lost already? I feel the excitement of something that has been found, but it is misshapen, uncertain. It is changing and I need to hold it tight.

I am heading for the big rock, where he seemed to stop so often. Surely that mark is his too?

The circle is still there, but faded, so very hard to see. I can feel it, tracing smooth skin over rough rock. Before I left the house this morning I found some bright red chalk in a cupboard of torches, batteries, and cleaning chemicals. Taking it out of my jacket, I trace over the circle to re-mark, feeling the friction as the colour rubs off on my fingers, listening to it grind and scrape.

I'll mark the other places too, on the trees and the rocks, and on the sketches I've started making in my notepad, my beginnings of maps. Redrawing where Dad was, before he fades completely. That might help.

FOUND HIS PAGES

FOUND YOURS

HELPED HIM AND HELP YOU

HELP YOU FIND DARKNESS

Today was running away and running towards. I kept turning for her, looking over my shoulder for a comforting presence, for a reassurance that wasn't there. Each time was a surprise, and yet it kept repeating. I kept repeating.

The same is happening over and over, but I don't seem to be learning from any of these failures. I am looking at everything all wrong. I am looking

99

back when I need to look forward, to find what is ahead. That is where she is waiting.

The sky was clouded today, its weak blue hiding and barely seen. Layers of grey upon grey, blown over each other, rolling and pushing on.

5.17pm. Wind, rain starting.

OPEN

MOUNTAIN SKY OPEN

CLOSED

THINKING CLOSED

QUESTIONS CLOSED

MUM DAD DEAD CLOSED

QUIET

CALM VOICE

CALLING YOU LITTLE BIRD

LITTLE DEAD BIRD

5.

There's a change in the air, a difference now I've climbed higher. I saw nothing else on the way up. No people and no more chalk marks.

I can see the sun sliding past its own summit. Time to up and move and start to come back down from the mountaintop, even if I don't want to. To leave a few distant golden eagles floating and waiting.

Walking back down, I'll pass the big rock again. I can check that faded circular mark. Then I can follow from there, explore other routes and see what else I can find, what else hasn't disappeared yet.

I keep coming back to the fixation Dad had with hiding, with the idea that his dead wife was being hidden somewhere nearby. My Mum. Hidden by a devil that lurks in the hollow, where the ground seems to have given way, where the mountain has collapsed into itself.

I'm moving very slowly down from the peak, looking hard at where you could hide here, and finding it all more confusing than ever. This is a place to get lost in bad weather, caught off guard, but today in all of the brightness everything feels open. Everything is on show: rough, worn trails, the big loch, the sea just showing at the horizon's edge, the other peaks that rise, that cluster together. The ragged shapes of wilderness.

Moving always brought joy to Mum and Dad, but there is no joy to be found here, not now, not yet. What is hard is how much healing I need, how massive and ferocious it is, how impossible to see the distance it reaches. I can feel it without looking but I want to look, I want to understand, I want to be able to measure any improvement, any change, just as he did.

> *If the Devil is tricking me with beauty, what else am I wrong about? Everything here is layers, some real, some not. It is bright now, which feels comfortable. Maybe that is a trick too.*

I feel quiet and small. I haven't seen anyone I know in such a long time, but I haven't missed anyone either, apart from Mum and Dad. My isolation, my loneliness is pointed, specific – it is only the company of two people that could heal it. The company of anyone else would simply make it worse. My companions are the birds high in the sky and the faded chalk marks, those circles and crosses.

Sometimes you pass people out here, light-footed, buoyed by their achievements and endorphins. Sometimes it is easy to say hi as you pass. Sometimes it feels like chewing rocks.

Sometimes you think you know them, but don't.

That neon red jacket is with me again.

Time to stop thinking. To push out Mum and Dad and demons, and just step, step, step. Take those words from Dad. They are mine now.

QUIET

QUIET CALM

CALM NO MORE

AWAY AWAY

I'm lightly running now, eager to get back down to the big rock. The chalk marks feel like a new start, but I know I need to hold some caution, need to push back against the temptation to get carried away.

The ground is level enough for me to gather some speed, hearing the satisfying crunch of stone upon stone. As I approach the forest I can feel the brush of heather against my calves, rough even through the stretched running fabric.

The big rock is there, overlooking the ocean of trees below. Once again I'm following his footsteps, as this place repeats in the notes so many times. Nearer, I can see what a comfortable position this is, a point from which to look out on all that is below.

I lean against it, trying to find the circle. The smoothness is still there, the gap in the lichen's growth, but no mark. No red mark from earlier. Has it rained? Not at the top, but maybe it did here. The weather changes so fast, so often that I can't be sure. It feels dry. I get out my chalk and draw my circle on it again, dismissing the doubt, wondering where else he marked and tested, what else he was looking for.

I have tried to mark each tree, but there is no need. I'm spreading further now, building a grid, taking in more. There is always more.

103

The gentle slope pulls me into the trees, and I pause. The sound changes, the wind no longer free to roam but caught between trunks and branches, aching and whistling, its movement always given away, always betrayed.

Is that another mark, low on the tree trunk? He must have been crouching to draw there. What else was he looking at? The rock had a circle, but this seems to be a cross. I turn – the two are in sight of each other, if that helps. Are these being mapped against each other, linked, measured in some way?

Why this tree? Why one Scots pine among so many thousands? It looks the same as every other one I can see: thin-trunked, reaching up to the sky, uneven branches stretching out and holding clouds of dark green needles.

I draw over the cross in my red chalk and move on, deeper in, my back to the rock and the mountain. The ground is smoother here, with a softness and spring underfoot.

> Some marks wash off in the rain, some don't. I can feel this tension, this change as I move around the forest. There is activity here but not there. Safety there but not here.

There seem to be more, but I stop to be sure. There seems to be a random mixture of crosses and circles, all at waist height or lower. I'm puzzled that I've not seen these before, even on my way out of the forest earlier today. But they are all facing towards the peak, so they could have been hidden on the opposite side of the tree trunks, watching my back as I left. I mark them again.

104

My chalk rubs against the papery surface of another Scots pine, catching the ridges between grey plates of bark that burst into shining orange as the trunk rises to the canopy. There are dozens of fresh chalk marks now.

Mark the trees, mark the maps. Watch for everything that can change.

I've covered some distance now, and can feel the chalk matted over my fingers as the thin red stick has got smaller and smaller, then crumbled to nothing. I stop and listen for the river by the cottage but realise I can't hear its steady roar. I stand still and hold my breath. Where am I?

I turn and turn, but can see nothing to guide me. In every direction are only the same tree trunks, thousands of them repeating and repeating. The forest suddenly feels crowded, flat, a wall of bark closing in.

I listen, but still nothing. I start walking to try and find the last tree I marked, but I'm struggling, panic rising. Then I remember they are all facing the way I came in. Looking to the mountain. I am facing the wrong way.

I must have come back into the forest a slightly different direction, being taken away from the cottage, from the route I always drive in. Now I am seeing things anew.

My footsteps have lightly stirred the forest floor, just enough to help me catch the end of the thread I've lost. But it is slow, finding a red circle or cross, then looking around and seeing no more, then checking the opposite side of the next tree, and on, and on, and on. This will take hours to unpick. I've no idea where the marks were leading me.

For now, it's enough to try and stop getting lost, to slowly creep back to the forest's edge and then try to find my way back in again.

There is no pattern yet, and maybe there will never be. The marks may each be alone too.

LISTEN

LISTEN

LONELY

LISTEN

I found the cottage, eventually, still startled by how far I'd travelled, how totally engrossed I'd become in the chase, never thinking of where I was heading, never worrying how little attention I was paying to everything else around me.

This isn't new, this obsessive streak, this blinkered way of trying to navigate the world. I have seen it in myself, and again and again in others drawn to movement, others like me.

Once you reach a point of trying and enjoying an outdoor pursuit then you are lured in quickly and suddenly. You are consumed. There is passion, guilt, and cheating. Cheating time from those you love, and cheating more from life than it feels fair to take.

For me it is all about escape. That feeling is worth risking almost anything. I know Mum and Dad saw things differently, saw a beauty in steadiness and security, even while taking considerable risks out here, but for me the pull is to something else. I want to be alone, flying down a mountain, riding a wave of gravity, mud, and loose rocks, trainer soles tapping on and off the tide as it bucks and wrests and wrenches. I want to be the wind.

And what I will do to chase that sensation defies any reasonable explanation. If you don't share this obsession, then you can't understand it – words are not enough to bridge that lack of experience. Driving hundreds of miles, waking in the middle of the night, gritting teeth through needle-sharp rain: all are normal. All are, very simply, worth it. Worth it for fractions of time that make me me.

But, despite the joy, a frustration still burns. It is achieving more than others and less than some, it is climbing a tall mountain and knowing of a taller one, it is learning and practising and enduring enough to know every way in which I fail. It is seeing the cracks in glorious success. It is always and never enough.

I don't know if I have everything wrong, but I've met lots of others who share similar stories. Obsessives with injuries and failures and joy and long, long lives woven with pointless, self-imposed challenges. No one made us climb these mountains, or scream down them as if possessed. No one is hunting us, but still we run.

And still we chase ghosts through forests, never really asking why.

DARKNESS COMING

FIRE AND FIRE

AND DARKNESS COMING

6.

Mum loved maps, but I never learnt to read them properly. I can follow what a map means, match the rippling contour lines to a slope and a peak, at least when I am inside and safe. Or inside, even if I am not safe, even if it still feels like the trees are watching and the branches are conspiring, whispering, talking of what comes next.

When I am outside it all unravels. My points of reference warp, my view shifts, and disorientation quickly follows. I go the wrong way. So when I run I tend to trace well-worn paths or repeatedly follow routes I already know, that I have tentatively learnt by exploring, getting lost. Memories scratched out of dead ends and retraced steps.

Dad could follow a map but didn't have the same passion for them as Mum, for their art and technical precision, for their unchanging truth. That they are always the same, whatever the light, whatever the weather. To Dad they were tools of location and rescue, to be checked before you left and then only again if things went wrong. Otherwise, they were a barrier to what was around you, an abstraction that got in the way of experiencing the mountains themselves. Putting paper between yourself and the world.

Dad never drew or painted at home, but here in the cottage there are sketches of hills and paths, of things he noticed on his walks. Maps, of sorts, quite unlike the map that drew me here.

Today I want to find them all. I empty all the boxes, spread out their contents, ready to excavate again. Unlike the writing, some of these images do seem to have been drawn outside, presumably while moving and searching for Mum, while others are neater, with sharper lines and uncreased pages. They are all minimal, practical, definitely not attempts at any sort of art. They are timid, reaching out, looking for connections.

I followed the dot from the attic, from their old weather-beaten map of these hills to find this empty, lonely forest and these empty, lonely pages. To find where that photograph of Mum was taken. His maps may have once connected the pages of writing to each other, but no longer.

SKETCHING

SCRATCHING

FINDING

FADING

LOST

I am cold, cold through. The winter is biting. Today was frozen mud and iced rock. Every direction was slow.

Writing this is slow too, the words stuck. They need to warm, to melt a little, but can't.

I have a small fire, bare and apologetic in its grate, hardly even casting a shadow. It is colour and little more, the heat evaporating before it touches anything.

I will stop now. I have to stop.

7.27pm. Frozen.

Despite his focus, his attempts at precision, the few drawings I've found vary greatly. Some appear to be traditional top-down maps, indicating the river and the forest's edge, the ridge of peaks behind. Others are pictures with a point of view, rough outlines of the mountains seen from below. A few are ripped into pieces, torn in frustration, either at an inability to translate his imagination to the page, or anger at the months of pointless searching. At being no closer to her.

It's hard to make any sense of these almost-maps, with their sharp pencil lines and vague shapes. Some clearly connect one place to another, suggesting a route he had taken or intended to take. Perhaps retracing them in another light, other weather, a different time of day. Once again his obsession with repeating and repeating, with seeing the world new and changed. With finding her, if only everything would come back together, if only everything would be just right again.

I am tired now, really tired. I've been running through these pages for hours, the boxes spread across the cottage floor, spilling open, but I've only found a dozen or so of the sketches. They are streaked with uneven, faltering lines, dotted with meandering paths, and entirely without words. Lines, dots, and a few circles and crosses that must mark important places, viewpoints, possibilities to explore further. They look like the markings I found chalked on the trees. But nothing more, nothing to attach any of the maps to any of his endless words.

Actually, I'm wrong. I'd missed this before but, unlike the notes, some of the maps are sketched on both sides of the page. These seem to be the rougher, creased pieces of paper, the ones I'm sure he drew outside while searching, rather than remembering and recording afterwards. The neat paper is single-sided, more considered, more composed.

The outdoor drawings are pretty much the same as each other, except one. One stands out. A quickly sketched pencil map with a single word, tiny but almost engraved on the page. I turn it over in the weak light from the window, and see that he pressed so hard while writing he almost ripped through the paper. Looking closely, the word shows on both sides, embossed and urgent. Repeatedly written over itself.

One word, sitting near a stack of twisting contour lines, wedged just past the side of a severe slope.

One word.

Hotel.

This morning was better, a little better. I woke ready to forget yesterday, to move on again, to find something new, inside and outside. There must be more, always more to find. Much that I have not seen, or seen and not understood.

I have spent a lot of time thinking about what she would have done here, where she might have gone, both then and now. Then it was youthful love and gleeful adventure. Now it is not, but it is still her, it is still these unreliable, shifting mountains. Something must remain, even when everything else is lost.

I am trying to retrace where we went back then, knowing this is impossible, but also knowing that I am crossing our paths wherever I go, whether I try to or not. We are still here, always a step or two ahead, a step or two behind.

We tried to visit that hotel once. We wanted to walk in, to feel the glow of the grand fireplaces and take a drink. We changed into our neatest, cleanest clothes, walked and walked through the woods, nervous and excited, only to pull up just short.

Neither of us knew wealth, what it feels like, how it has its own violence. Seeing the kilted men and fur-coated women stepping out of cars as we emerged from the trees, hearing them roar like fires, already full of fine wine, was a hurricane to us. We simply couldn't get near them. We took a step back and watched, silently.

No one saw us, but still we felt the humiliation. Turning, without a word, we started our long walk back.

I must go back there, try again, but it is darker now.

6.14pm. Wind carrying.

Why hotel? Which hotel? He mentioned something like this in other notes, some of the first notes I found, but then it felt like an aside, one of so many hundreds of similar comments, hidden in all the talk of a devil and the hollow and my poor, trapped Mum. Not important enough to be scored into the page, almost bursting through.

Here there are no hotels, only the occasional bed and breakfast dotted around for hikers looking to tick a remote summit off their list. The nearest actual hotel is well over an hour's drive away, on the way to a larger town, where civilisation reassembles itself after being blown apart on the peaks.

I returned today.

Now the hotel windows are all covered in chipboard, but it was badly done. Rushed, as if it needed to be finished in a hurry. Keeping in and keeping out.

The rain has also crept in, softening the edges, revealing corners of window frames. Slowly, patiently peeling layers away.

I went back and walked cautiously around the hotel. I looked for gaps and cracks, wondering what it might look like inside.

There was nothing, nothing but threat. I felt it there more strongly than anywhere so far.

4.52pm. Stormy.

I've turned back now to the map that brought me here, from the attic to the forest, from the attic to a dot. I am scouring that map for anything that resembles a hotel, a building, the outline of a structure that he could have meant.

I am trying to connect his uneven lines to the military precision of the Ordnance Survey mapping, looking for echoes from one to the other, but can find nothing. There is nothing.

This matters, but I don't know why. I have to keep looking.

She was always so calm, kind, and gentle, but something changed in her that night. That the wilderness, this beautiful emptiness, had been taken and used, turned into something else, unsettled her deeply. That nature was not enough by itself, that it needed to be tamed and refined, presented on a silver platter. That part of the wilds would never be open to us.

We stalked back, night after night, for the rest of that trip. Firstly, just out of a dark curiosity, to watch the otherness of the people who stayed there, how doors were opened for them, how the stretching horizons held nothing but a passing, mild interest. Their privilege dragging after them like heavy clouds.

Then it became more. She wanted to go back in the dark, to throw stones at their windows from the safety of the trees. She joked about burning the place down, to teach them, to give it back to the wild and the wind. I couldn't see the limits of her playfulness clearly, couldn't tell how much she really meant it.

She spoke softly about everyone who had been cleared from these lands before, her ancestors who were forced to leave Scotland before returning generations later. Of the poison of wealth. A history I knew nothing of and my family didn't share.

The hotel came to mean something, something far more than what it was. I thought it was a harmless plaything, a place that gave a few people jobs at least, that brought money here rather than somewhere else. But for her, it was the death of wilderness, the death of nature and freedom.

That anger softened over time and it became a shared joke, a watchword. Whenever arrogance or entitlement threatened, whenever something was ridiculously out of place, or whenever either of us felt the need to step outside the rules and rebel a little, there was one word which instantly shared that feeling.

Our code word.

Hotel.

7.09pm. Fierce winds now.

LOOKING

FINDING

FAILING

FALL

7.

It's been a week or so since I last wrote, and I've read and read and read, in the cottage and outside when it's been warm enough, when the sunshine has briefly broken through. Any remaining heat from the autumn is rapidly fading, the wind sharpening with each day.

I'm going back to the piles of words, taking notes, placing pieces around me and waiting for patterns and sanity and kindness to emerge from somewhere. Each day I've taken a new route out to the forest or beyond, based on the previous day's reading and notes.

I tried to find more of the chalk marks but failed. I'm guessing they were just an attempt at creating a structure, a meaningless shape. What mattered was the endless marking, movement for its own sake. I've given up on that, for now at least.

I've found a few more of his maps, but none that give any helpful information, and none with any words bar that single confusing drawing of the hotel. I've also looked, in the words and the hills, for anything that could suggest or resemble what he was referring to.

I drove back to the Post Office to buy any different maps I could find of the area, at different scales or from different years, wondering if a structure might have been added or removed from the mapping at some point. Each day I've looked for any buildings I may have missed before, but have found nothing. For once, everything is the same as before. Nothing has changed.

I'm tracking invisible steps, but no longer thinking too hard about it. I'm trying not to get caught on the breathlessness of a suggestion, the agitation and excitement of that single page, that tiny clue that may mean nothing. I can't know what he was thinking then, what he might be thinking now.

Breathe and breathe. I've done this before, this game of getting carried away with nothing and for no reason. It's hard to recognise it, but I have to try. I have to let go. If the wind or the sunshine pulls me one way, I am trying to follow it. Not necessarily because there is anything to find, anything waiting at the end, but at least attempting a greater softness and calmness than before. Trying to be calm by acting calm.

Reading these hard words has to be about working towards healing and peace. It must, especially as I keep getting stuck and stuck again. I need to find that peace, and I know it will take a long time.

Most likely it will not happen here, but in a blank moment back home, far into the future. A sudden, small realisation that the grief has passed, or faded far enough into the distance to be indistinguishable from clouds and haze on the horizon.

I will start again and I will forget everything. I will find a way of moving beyond what I have seen, what I have thought. She is here but I have never glimpsed her, never found a clue, a moment, an opening.

I know she is here. She is here and held, and I can't see her. I love her and am failing her.

I sat by her hospital bed and failed her. Now she is here and I am failing her again.

Please know that every step is an act of love, every note, every attempt, no matter how weak and futile they are. No matter how much failure there is, how much of a failure I am, it is all love.

I love her, I love her, I love her. I will find her.

Tomorrow I begin again.

8.55pm. Rain starting.

This hurts. Of course it all hurts, but I think this is the only note I've read where he seems to connect to Mum's illness, where he mentions anything of what came before.

It's hard to know what he was thinking, what he perhaps is thinking still. Each morning I open the cottage door with the same fear, the same hope. Those impossible notes, that surely couldn't have been, that I know couldn't have been. Fearing more of them and yet hoping for more. Hoping for any connection to him, however terrifying, however hard to explain. I hope, but there is nothing.

This is my own failure. He was looking for her, he is still looking for her. I was looking for him, I am looking for him. It is all past, it is all now.

I am failing at something I can barely understand.

YES

LISTEN

MORE

MORE QUIET

MORE QUIET VOICE

MORE YOU

His last note is calling for a reply, for a reassurance. It is half of a conversation that can never be answered, can never be completed.

I should leave now, return to the house, get out of this suffocating forest and try to breathe again. Each time I leave I try to tidy a little before I go, so it is all neat and recognisable, so it is easier to tell if anything has been moved overnight. I know this is ridiculous, but still I do it.

There's one box that's almost emptied, with just a few pages left hidden at the bottom. For the sake of neatness, of completeness, I will finish those pages before I go.

I pick them all up, place them on the table and spread them out. Usually I scan over a few at a time, to see if there are any sketches, anything that immediately takes my attention. There's nothing but words on these notes.

Looking more closely, they're all split into sections. They all look very similar to each other. I think it's the first piece of writing that coherently lasts more than a few pages, and where I might be able to piece the pages together, to find the edges that fit, to give the words back their own momentum and flow.

These new pages read very differently, though I'm not clear when he wrote them. I think it was most likely in summer, judging by the times of the day. About halfway through his time here, after one of the many restarts, the multiple attempts to find some sort of scientific method to cool his fury and fear.

But, of course, it didn't last as long as he intended.

Today is where control starts. I set my alarm last night, got up, washed in cold water, ate, moved lightly around the cottage, stretched a little. Getting ready for the day ahead.

Each day I will do the same tests at the same time, with the same breaks in between. Every three hours, unless I have to travel very much further, which will come later. I will build up and build up. I will be ready then, but am not yet.

Start small. Step, step, step.

The order doesn't matter, but keeping the order does.

I will return after each test, rest and recover.

I will write all of this down, in the same way, immediately after each test.

Each day will be the same, until one test has been exhausted, something important proven or disproven.

I will watch the weather and the seasons change. The years change, if they have to. I will wait, patiently, ignoring the magical spells of sunlight and lightning strikes.

What matters is hidden behind that, it is smaller and quieter. It is in the texture of light, barely there, almost impossible to see.

It must be felt over time, with experience and calmness and focus. To find anything I must let myself go completely.

Day one.
08.00am. Test 1.
Forest, immediately around the cottage.

She matters, I do not matter. Rigour and discipline are everything now.

Cold, grey. Sunlight held back behind thick cloud. Wind blowing.

Chalk marks intact on the trees. Nothing moved, nothing changed.

11.00am. Test 2.
Forest, further from the cottage.

Still cold, some light seeping through the canopy, but not dripping down to the forest floor yet.

Wet underfoot from yesterday's rain. All of the sounds are different. Footsteps are dulled, not rustling.

Paused by the very edge of the forest in silence, breathing and waiting. Listening. I feel something here.

1.00pm. Test 3.
Lower hills, just beyond the forest edge.

Sun still struggling through. Scree drying, losing its shine and brilliance, dark metal fading to dull grey.

Buzzards soaring and crying over the treetops, then plunging into dense branches.

Nothing here but silence.

4.00pm. Test 4.
Midway up the hill, by the big rock.

Some warmth, faint sunshine, uncertain and timid.

Watching the trees swaying, brushing, whispering to each other. Sharing and conspiring. A conversation that has lasted centuries.

On a different day, a different conversation, a different tone.

7.00pm. Test 5.
The false peak, halfway up.

Harder to reach this climb than usual. I feel a little weak – noting this, because I am noting everything.

To find her is to watch everything and ignore everything. The Devil's influence could be everywhere, so it all matters. Watch, measure, record.

Listen.

10.00pm. Test 6.
The river that feeds the loch, at the opposite end of the forest.

Light fading. The river still sings, quietly, but with strength.

I sit and listen with every part of me, as the river runs and runs.

There is something here too, something resonates, but I must watch out.
This is beautiful, so it may be a trick. Let go, listen, wait.

Day two.
08.00am. Test 1.
Forest, immediately around the cottage.

Hard winds blew through overnight, trees tangled, branches grabbing each
other far overhead. The forest feels warped, out of shape.

Rain has streaked the chalk marks down the tree trunks. I re-mark,
carefully.

I am not sure what I am measuring, but the marking is routine and
pattern and a point to start from. The rain has dried on one side of the
trees, but not the other.

11.00am. Test 2.
Forest, further from the cottage.

Sun rising and wind calmed. The edge of this forest matters: it's where
shelter begins and ends. On one side, comfort and life, on the other, dark-
ness and death. But which is which is still hard to tell.

I sit, as close to silent as I can manage, until this block of time is nearly
done. There is more here, but I must return, record, prepare for the next test.

This place may be something, or a distraction from something.

1.00pm. Test 3.
Lower hills, just beyond the edge.

I have some strength back today. The slope feels shallower, easier.

I note this and let it go. It will soon be meaningless, just pieces of information blown around me. Leaves in a storm.

4.00pm. Test 4.
Midway up the hill, big rock.

Sitting, breathing, listening to the wind. It has rhythm again, confidence. It is preparing itself.

7.00pm. Test 5.
The false peak, halfway up.

Brighter and calmer now. I am watching the light, and stay here for well over an hour, unmoved.

There is a fascination in the edges of light, something I have always felt. I am drawn to these almost imperceptible moments of beauty. They feel safer than the grand sweeping views, the sunsets that cast wide and vulgar for everyone to see.

I think I am looking for imperfections. Minute flaws in the world around me, and perhaps in me too. The changes I'm looking for may take minutes, or may take months.

Breathe. My thoughts are gathering momentum. I am running out of time. I don't know if I have found something, or if the Devil has found another trick, subtler, cleverer this time.

Note it, move on, return.

10.00pm. Test 6.
The river, at the opposite end of the forest.

Some light still coming through, water glistening and shifting.

Singing its song. Drowning out the quieter noises nearby.

Day three.
08.00am. Test 1.
Forest, near.

I am struck by a moment of terror.

What if the Devil can read these notes?

Stop. Continue to test. Consistency is everything – other things can't be changed, and can't be helped.

11.00am. Test 2.
Forest, further.

Moving now, with rhythm.

I feel I am closer to something.

Tracing the edge, with energy and anger today.

Not sitting, watching, listening, but pacing, turning to running. Running up and down.

The ground is soft and uneven, rutted and rooted. Easy to turn and snap an ankle. Step light, listen.

Move, but move quickly.

1.00pm. Test 3.
Lower hills.

I stretched the area today, covered more ground.

Am I being drawn away from details, or am I seeing more, seeing a bigger picture?

Is the Devil reading this?

4.00pm. Test 4.
Midway up the hill.

She is here.

She is definitely here. I can feel it, there is something happening.

I have been wrong, again. I was too unstructured, then too detailed. Too big, then too small.

What is happening is between.

7.00pm. Test 5.
The false peak.

Stay in the middle, not too fast, not too slow.

Climb easily, scan from near to far, hold an easy focus. Lightness.

Noting, moving, slowly building rhythm.

A rhythm that can last.

10.00pm. Test 6.

The river.

This is it. This is the discovery, the real trick.

She is not hidden.

She is everything and everywhere.

She will not be found, but brought back together through moving, through momentum. I must continue to move, to take it all in.

And momentum is neither speed nor stopping. It is balance. The sprint and the meditation are both equally flawed and wrong. Both miss the middle.

I must repeat. I have found something and cannot, must not stop.

But what had he found? Not Mum, not me. He thought he was looking, but he was only running away.

This is enough. It is all enough. I understand less and less of him with each word. I love him less and less every day.

I could burn all of this, walk away, and never look back.

DAY ZERO
08.00AM. YOUR FIRST TEST

DAY

WATCHING

DAY

WAITING

11.00AM. YOUR SECOND TEST

THINGS TO SEE HERE

AND THINGS TO LOOK PAST

1.00PM. YOUR THIRD TEST

WARMING

SUNSHINE

BEAUTY WASHES OVER YOU

4.00PM. YOUR FOURTH TEST

RELAX

DON'T LOOK

DON'T LISTEN

7.00PM. YOUR FIFTH TEST

A DAY DONE

MOVED AND MOVED

10.00PM. YOUR FINAL TEST

LISTENING

LOOKING

128

SLIP AND MISS

HIDE

YOU LOST HER

QUIET AND ALONE

STOP THEN START

THEN STOP

STOP

STOPPED

Dusk

1.

We all have devils, pushing and pulling us, gently leading us one way or the other. Not the Devil, fallen, a rich fiction of evil and revenge, but softer, subtler forces steering us away from choosing the right thing, from persisting through difficulties. From being a better person.

I think of devils like weather, sometimes light winds guiding you, sometimes storms screaming in your face. But always challenging, nagging, undermining what you really want to do. Small darknesses that cloud who you are.

My own devil is doubt, doubt that can slide so easily into depression. It is usually quiet and calm, sometimes belligerent and fierce, but always waiting. Waiting for a moment of weakness, the smallest opportunity to pounce. I think it has always been there.

I remember one of the earliest moments coming face-to-face with this strange force, this hidden part of me. A school trip, hillwalking over moors, trampling heather underfoot. The occasional cry of surprise when firm ground gave way to collapsing bog, filling a child's walking boot with shockingly cold water.

And I was straying slightly away from the group, from my teachers, following a trail of thoughts. Pulled along by a bird's call and a fascination to find the creature, the image that matched the sound. A brief, harmless hunt.

The moment shifted, a change in the wind. I felt pulled along, a voice inside me encouraging every step. The bird was on the other side of a bump in the moorland, just hidden, just beyond the wide open plain where everyone could see everyone, where the group dispersed was still a group. A little further, and a little further.

Each single step was safe and innocent, incidental. At no point did I step over a cliff, or turn and break an ankle. But each step I took added momentum, building and building, the quiet voice slowly, ever so slowly getting harder and louder. Calling me to keep going, to keep going, on and on.

To a rise in the land, and over the smallest of crests. A slight downhill, then the ground flattened. I stood still, but couldn't hear a thing. No birdcall, no school group, no wind. Everything had stopped.

I felt in that moment a coldness, but no fear. There was a vague sense that I might have done something wrong, but no emotion behind this. No feeling. I have felt that coldness many times since, when hurting people, disappointing or leaving them, and here in these forests and mountains too. I am separate, or have been separated from something. Here I am cold and distant from myself.

The school trip ended badly. I felt that I had been away for minutes, but there was more to it than that. The memories blur, unreliable at this distance and marred by the emotion of it all. Not of the moment itself, but of everything around it. Of how it grew.

There were tears and shouting, blame and anger. I remember whistles being blown across the moor, and thinking what a strange sound that was out in the wild, so distinct, so unnatural. To this day whenever I hear that piercing noise, whether for a departing train or blown by a referee, I feel a stab of guilt.

The frantic whistles were soon joined by shouts, blending and blur-ring, a mess of panic. Young, high-pitched voices. Shrill, pleading teachers. People I knew, some I liked, swept away by their imagi-nations, by a terror of injury or death, of responsibility.

I wandered back over at some point and was found, apparently long, long after I'd left. The details are still fogged, fragmented. I recall that coldness, of walking back to the group as if I'd strayed into someone else's nightmare, and certainly not returned to a situation I had broken. There was talk of hypothermia, a rustling silver space blanket, my settled confusion at everyone's hysteria explained away as shock, but throughout I was clear: I had gone for a walk to find a bird. I said nothing of the voice, that secret part of me calling me on.

Pleading looks, knowing smiles, sympathetic noises and empty words. My trip swiftly cut short, parents rushing up to the hills, fraught with worry.

Mum and Dad were almost always calm, often irritatingly so. When I craved a reaction, kind silence usually came. But on that day they showed a raw, animal impulse, a violence driven by pure love. The most confusing of things for a child. That day fear and love boiled into anger.

But I had just been pulled along, quietly and calmly, by that hard voice.

The sun is setting now, but it is still early.

The sky bright, as the land and trees darken and fade.

In every moment a difference.

4.07pm. Some rain, wind growing.

All of his pages are out of order again. A cloud that came together, took shape briefly, then stretched, broke, and faded.

I have started to work through the remaining boxes of paper, shuffling them from the floor to the table and back. That long note has left me wanting to find any other pages that match together, that say anything about the attempts at more structured testing. At least, his version of that, in his darker and then darkest moments. They appear to be neat boxes, carefully divided, but within they are chaos, rolling words that lead nowhere.

Those detailed tests definitely started partway through his stay, long before the darkness really took over, long before he left for the last time, disappeared and died somewhere in these hills. His departure, that ending, feels like a starting point, another beginning for grief.

His ending, I assume. His death, I assume. I need to know something, anything. I need something solid to build from.

I am feeling the need for more structure, much the same as he did. I am also struck by what he wrote about the middle, of finding some balance between extremes. This has given me pause. Taken away from the strange context of hallucinations, and an imagined devil, it feels like a solid observation, wise even.

I have never been balanced in this way. Challenges are my oxygen and to be without them is to suffocate. I need things to achieve, to complete, and will seek these out wherever I am, whether they are there or not. I am always craving structure.

There are so many situations I have broken like this. Where no rules exist, or are ever required. Where a friend just needed me as me and nothing else was relevant. Where I should have been listening, not telling, and certainly not lecturing, pushing. But I was always looking for tiny opportunities to do more, do better, asking the same of everyone close to me. Demanding and improving. A blast zone waiting to happen.

It took so many years for me to understand why this situation would repeat and repeat, why strain would grow, relationships creak and crack, then irreparably break. Particularly where my advice hadn't been asked for, and likely wasn't wanted, but I'd still provided it with force. Thorough, detailed, excessive. Always too much, even if there were good ideas in there somewhere. There was always kindness lying behind this, kindness given but rarely received.

The kindness was based on simple, stupid assumptions: that everything needs to be completed, every possibility to improve must be acted upon, with energy and haste. That no moment is ever to be lost.

I feel in some pain writing this, the words coming more slowly now.

I do understand, with years and perspective, how destructive this was to almost everyone. Not to Mum and Dad who managed, entertained, distracted, and side-stepped my vicious enthusiasm. But to anyone else, anyone unwitting, there was a steady pattern. A relationship built, then needs shared, perhaps a job opportunity, a half-imagined personal goal, an academic challenge, a dream. Then came the growing thunder, the rapid momentum building in my brain. Taking the bit between my teeth, then always trying to bite through.

I broke so many things, so many people like this. Perhaps that's why no one is missing me now. Perhaps that's why Dad ran away, after my shouting. That day might have finally been the step too far.

But the comfortable balance others seem to have, focusing on life as and when they please, feels like a fiction to me. It is something I can't see, and can barely imagine.

Now I find myself doing the same with Dad's notes, spending hour upon hour reading, trying to put together anything that matches, looking for themes, links, words that match maps or maps that match words. Now I've started, I have to build a way through, creating structure even if there is none and even if it doesn't help. I just can't stop.

YOUR VOICE

LISTEN

QUIET AND LISTEN

MOVE AND STOP

I manically shuffle pages, piling and ordering, then sorting and reordering, always feeling that something is getting nearer, always feeling that a discovery is just one more step away, one more moment of gritted teeth and perseverance through doubt and exhaustion. It must be close, it must be. I push on and on, slipping further and further from the coldness of the dark cottage, the plain wooden seat, and the wind that is always reaching for me, howling through every crack it can find in the walls.

I need to let this go. I need to put the boxes down and step out of the cottage, find myself again on the slopes, but with each day that passes I spend longer and longer inside.

I need to move. That's really the only way I've ever felt any balance, by turning the mental excitement into motion. But even that gets caught in the push for more, for quicker, for harder and harder and harder, until one evil has simply been replaced by another.

At the other extreme is the deathly inertia that can grip me, those moments of vacuum and silence. Colours are emptied. Cold grey fire burning slowly inside me.

I need to remember to breathe, then remember to move. Step, step, step, as Dad wrote over and over again. To conjure up some small motion that lifts my heart rate, carrying more oxygen around my body, the beginnings of rediscovering my own momentum. Gradually, softly, slowly.

To glide smoothly, to find a comfortable pace between frozen terror and a death sprint is the only challenge I don't know how to start.

I am still sat in the cottage. I haven't moved.

QUIET NOW

QUIET AND DARK

THE DARKNESS IS YOU

NOTHING BUT DARKNESS

My own words are irritating me now.

I want to stop. I want all of this to stop.

I feel the need to scream, to scream at myself. At my incompetence and being so completely powerless. At the way I'm sitting in a ruined cottage day and night, piecing crazed fragments back together, holding back grief. Looking, searching for something, someone, a surely lost someone.

I want to yell at that neon red jacket, neon red jacket, neon red jacket. At those impossible notes, left when they could not be left.

At that voice, that quiet voice that pushes me and pushes me, to move, to stop, to break people and break myself, to fail over and over again. I don't want to listen any more.

I hate this so much.

LISTEN

LISTEN

LISTEN TO YOUR VOICE

QUIET VOICE

BURNING VOICE

DARK

DARK

NOW

This evening was beautiful beyond anything I can describe. I wish I could draw or paint, to give even a weak impression of its wonder.

I woke, went straight out and climbed, felt the warmth coming to me as I moved. Feet crunching, snapping the silence, past the forest, up the early rises, to the first false summit and beyond. A long, slow day outside. I can't remember when that last happened.

And at the end of it the winter sun set the ground and sky on fire, slowly, achingly. Reds and yellows, turning to dark. A sky that would have impressed Turner.

For a moment I almost forgot everything else, almost forgot her. For that, I am so, so sorry.

5.43pm. Frozen, everything shining.

I am outside again, needing to feel something. It is cold and I am poorly dressed. I am deliberately unprepared. I don't deserve to be safe.

I am cold now, feeling the wind wrapping me, fingers numbing, heat escaping, starting to shiver, that fluttering in your chest when it's craving heat, burning energy, running you closer to empty. I want to feel this. I want it to hurt.

There are dark thoughts coming in. I can feel how they brush against me, testing, sensing how much I react, how far they can push before I notice, before I push back. Brushing, then retreating. Brushing, then retreating. Their sharp edges coming closer and closer.

My fingers are throbbing now, my whole body cooling, my face stinging, and I am waiting and watching.

The light is fading, my brain is not.

The air is cold and I am burning.

7.14pm. On the edge of night.

I am dancing around something, but don't know if I should.

He felt that same pull to experiment. Not to hurt or risk himself on purpose, I'm sure, but testing every limit in his total commitment to finding Mum. A necessary step on the way to rescuing her.

It's calling to me too. It is coming closer, or I am getting closer to it. He repeated and repeated, he tried to find some sort of method to make sense of all of this.

It strikes me that I've never done the same. Is this a failure? Was he more committed to finding Mum than I am to finding him? Is he still? Is, was, is, was. That neon red jacket again. Those impossible notes again.

I can't write any more. I love you.

I want to look so closely at the sun that it is extinguished. I want everything to burn until it can burn no more.

I must stop now. Everything must stop now.

2.

It's been a few days now, a few days of moving little and writing nothing. I have doubted everything in every moment. I have kept coming back to the cottage, stayed longer, wondered more about staying here, sleeping here, about letting go of my fear of the forest. I have resisted this urge, tried to resist, but what does it matter anyway? My own devil has been quietly whispering.

The clouds always come in swiftly, but silently. It doesn't show to anyone else, bar my inability to smile quite so quickly at a joke or a kind comment. Now I've learnt to fake the smile after years of careful practice, but there is still a flicker, the tiniest delay that can barely be spotted unless you know. Unless you feel that deep pain too.

Outside, nothing. Inside, a storm. It boils within me and the rage grows and grows. Rolling clouds, darkening above. Pure energy, anger with no foundation, no purpose, and no outlet. A neat, violent circle, spinning with ever-increasing momentum.

My devil is quiet. It doesn't announce itself. It doesn't declare a war that must be fought, trumpet into battle. It is cunning, lithe, and secretive. It's taken me years to realise its permanent presence, to be watchful and ready. To expect it.

Now I must expect it more than ever. I must be ready and waiting, just as it is.

The light is magical later in the afternoon, as it changes and changes.

It begs you to stay and watch, to look closely and slowly. To hold your gaze and stop thinking. To let time move around you, not waiting for anything.

She was always the most incredibly patient person, who could find beauty and wonder in the smallest moment. Pausing, on a walk, catching sight from distance of a twitch in the heather or the tree line, breathing softly, dead still, waiting for a creature to show itself, after its own fears of predator and prey have faded.

Sometimes we would walk and walk for hours, barely stopping, and other times we would stop and stop, barely managing to walk. Those short walks were intense and wonderful, seeing the world in another way, seeing things that felt like they had never existed before, or would not have existed without the simple act of looking.

She taught me this, to look, and how to look. Once I'd learnt how, I always marvelled at most people being incapable of looking up and seeing the sky in a city, full of clouds unconcerned for where they cast their passing shadows, or unable to look out of a train window as they rush through fields and along coastlines, as the land shifts and morphs around them.

For a while I commuted by train, crossing farmland, rising to higher ground that was prone to snow in winter, before falling back down again.

I have vivid memories of staring out of the windows of those trains, seeing deer straying from the shade of wooded copses, grazing in fields on foggy, frosty mornings, as everyone inside our carriage tapped on screens. Scrolling and scrolling, ticking away time. Our two worlds not touching each other.

I always longed to be part of that other world, and with her. Not behind the glass looking out, and certainly not outside looking in. To be so far gone that everyone trapped inside, framed by glazing and heating and comfort, doesn't even know we exist. To be entirely elsewhere, and of something else.

6.12pm. Back inside now. Calm.

I am still nowhere in these words, and have now stopped looking. There are thousands more pages that I will never read, could never read, but I don't imagine I'm in any of them either.

This is what I get, for what I did to him. This is what I deserve.

At the start this hurt, piling grief upon grief, but now it is just a curiosity, an accepted fact.

PAGES HIDDEN

SHUFFLING

EVER SHUFFLING

I stayed away from the cottage today, back at the house. I'm no longer sure why I'm here, living alone deep in the Highlands. It has been many weeks now and finally might be time to go back.

But I'm not sure how to go back, or where I want to go back to.

I should have gone for a run, forced myself up and out the door, but I couldn't. My back hurt a little, I told myself, and I felt a slight ache on the inside of one knee. Surely it would hurt to move, maybe it's better to rest, maybe it's better just to stay here, just this once. What does one day matter?

I never left. Today barely moved, the curtains stayed closed for the morning and well into the afternoon. The rain came on again. I heard it first, then watched it painting lines down the window in my tiny lounge. A small sofa, yellowing walls, a framed square of scruffy garden, fenced in by the wild glories of nature all around. Cornered, contained, like I am.

Trapped in circles, tracing the route from the sofa to the fridge, sometimes to the toilet, and back again.

I can't write any more just now.

TALKING

YOUR QUIET VOICE

WHISPER

WHISPER

LISTEN

It's been weeks here now. How many, I'm not even sure.

I can feel the urge to do something, to be somewhere else, someone else, but the weight holding me down is too strong. That endless pressure.

Remember, remember, remember. This isn't new. This comes and this goes, this comes from nowhere but it can go, it has gone before, whatever might be happening now. Remember. Please try to remember.

Remember to keep moving, to never stop moving.

But I have already stopped. To start, I need to do something. One thing. To break the routine, my settled routine that is holding, suffocating, dragging me down with it.

Phone. I have lived so long now without my phone, without even thinking about it, when back home I could barely manage minutes. I feel sick at everything it might hold, all of the echoes inside.

Not to contact anyone, or to expect anything from them, but to see that other people are out there, with lives and news and joy and misery. Remembering others, no matter how far away. Remembering that they hurt too.

In the forests and mountains there is no phone signal, no hope of it at all. Here among the little cluster of houses it drips through, just enough to listen in on the rest of the world.

I charge my phone, as it has been dead for weeks. I turn it on and open the front door – where has night come from? I step out, to try and find a bar or two, madly walking up the street, reaching for an invisible signal, craving a moment of connection.

Past the houses, as the copse of lamp-posts ends, it connects. The phone screen bright in the coming winter darkness, searching, searching. It is slow, but it starts.

A few missed calls I can ignore, numbers I know and numbers I don't, and one message. From a colleague, a kind colleague. Perhaps reaching out. It's a surprise to hear from her. I feel an unfamiliar rush of warmth, but as I open the message it jars. This wasn't what I was expecting. The message is short, sharp, pointing to an email. A must read, I'm sorry, so sorry, given everything else.

What? The email takes much longer to load, as I pace along the side of the road, a petrol tanker roaring past, taking the Highland roads at speed in darkness, with somewhere else to be.

I frantically skip over screens and screens of newsletters, receipts, and reminders, to find the only thing I'm looking for. It is another horror, sprung from nowhere.

What I built out there, what I had waiting for me to come back to, has gone. I took a break and now there is nothing.

Administrators, restructuring, creditors to be paid, a difficult time, the industry is moving on. We're so sorry, but. We tried everything we could, but.

I have nothing left to return to. I turn off.

DARKNESS

DARKNESS

COMING

NOW

I'm not sure if I slept.

I sat by the window for a while, feeling the weakness of the new morning. Outside, the trees stood firm on the slopes, one behind the other. Always there, in sun and rain and darkness, standing and waiting. Watching.

Mostly I sat doing nothing, just staring out, blankly. Not looking, just stuck. There was no movement today, no hope of finding any momentum. Slow and slow and stuck.

A deer jumped the fence at one point. Young, tentative, head twitching and smelling the air around it. It nibbled at the grass, softly combing over the unkept garden, always drawn back to the raw nature around it. Nibbling, then head jumping up, alert, quivering. Then back down, then a sound, and head back up again. Over and over.

What a way to live: eating, then frightened, then eating, then frightened. Constantly checking for death.

A car door slammed outside one of the other houses and the deer simply, effortlessly bounded back over the fence. A white tufted tail disappearing into the trees, then there was nothing to show it had been there at all.

I sat.

150

LISTENING

LISTENING

QUIET VOICE

THIS IS YOU

LISTEN

I took a slow walk today. Step, stop, breathe. At each point looking down, around, and up, looking near and far, watching how the world changes in a single step.

As a child I was baffled by forests, by the way the layers of trees slide past each other as you watch them. It was worse moving at speed in our car. I'd follow each tree with my eyes as far as I could, absorbed, skipping back and forth, trying to discern patterns, rhythms that can't last.

I am remembering things now, things that seem out of place now that she is gone, now that I have lost her. I am remembering quietness, how to breathe and listen to the breath. The almost silent rhythm of your own body, ticking away, hidden behind the rush of everyday life.

Watching and listening. Today's walk had dried leaves blowing over the path, trees kissing and jilting each other, playing games. A gentle wind chased itself around me, trying not to touch, to remain silent and unseen, but failing and softly grazing my cheek and forearm.

I am torn. Are these tricks, diversions? Should I be more on guard, more angry?

But I'm not angry at all. I feel a difference, the beginnings of some sort of peace. A small silence.

She is still out there, I'm sure.

11.00am. Light wind.

This is all too much for me. Everything is too heavy.

Slow.

Slow and nowhere to go.

Hard for the words to come, sometimes.

He is here, he is not here. Both are terrible.

She is not here.

Slow, painful words, again.

Each word a mile. Each sentence an hour, two, three.

Slow, slow, slowly hurting.

TIME TO BE WRONG

TORN AND BROKEN

SLOW

SLOW

STOP

What good is this? What does any of it matter?

I am standing on the front step of the house, looking out to the night. I needed to get out here, to breathe the air.

The few lamp-posts create tiny clouds of light, miniature bursts of brightness, making everything around them even darker, even harder to consider.

The air is cold, but still. The rain has passed to other peaks, other glens.

I see the occasional car, the headlights showing long before any sound reaches me. Watching the beams appear and disappear as the roads bend, tracing the loch edge or jumping behind trees. At this height trees can survive, in the relative shelter.

Nothing is straightforward here. There are no straight lines, except in air, except in water.

Maybe I will stay. Where else is there?

Perhaps I had it all wrong, perhaps I've been lying to myself. I am guiltier than I'd like to think. I can see a little more clearly, now my job has gone and life outside of these mountains is over. He came here because of me.

What could be left, after what I did?

If she is lost, it is because I lost her. I am missing this, it is being hidden from me all over again.

I felt calm, peaceful, settling over these past few days, accepting. But this is wrong, this is wrong, this is wrong.

I need to be angry and alert. I need to be finding, not waiting. Looking, searching, out there.

Looking across the forests I can see water vapour, rising and curling. Does that tell me something, give away a location, a change, a possibility?

Looking to the ridges where the clouds are blown upwards, turning over themselves, being shaped and compressed until they float off the top, formed, changed.

Looking, looking, looking. I need to be looking, or I will never find her. She is here, I know she is here.

3.06pm. Clouds and light.

That conversation, those burning words, keep coming back to me. I'm trying to stop it, but can't. Hours and days of this. It was months ago, but it is right now.

Dad and I are sitting in their living room, days after her funeral, with everything we hadn't said. With the terrible weight of silence choking us.

He sits, saying nothing, not moving, just looking back.

His eyes are open, pained like a child in the moment of shock before the explosion of tears. But tears never come.

I have taken all the air from the room, all of the sound, and left nothing for him. No way to respond, no way to make a connection, to apologise, to cry, to heal.

I have to leave the room, as he can't.

This is your fault.

Why didn't you?

Why didn't you take her to the doctor earlier, straight to the hospital, take a second opinion, a third?

I can hear myself speak, but don't recognise my own voice.

Why did you give up, as you always give up?

Why did you let the world happen to her, to take her from us?

She is dead because of you.

I am almost enjoying this now, letting my pain out, freeing it.

It is so loud.

This is your fault.

This is your fault.

And now I know I've broken everything between us.

I have to leave the room, as he can't.

ENOUGH

ENOUGH CALM QUIET

ENOUGH SLOW

BURNING NOW

I said all of those things, those things that were not true.

Nothing was his fault, now everything is mine.

He didn't kill her, but maybe I killed him.

Killed by my anger.

Killed by my grief.

NOW LIGHTNING RAGE

FIRE BURN

NOW YOU BURN TOO

3.

This morning felt different, maybe a bit better, maybe not, but definitely different. Less fog, less slowness, an energy returning. Dark nights and bright mornings, as Dad said. Thawing.

I know now what I did, how wrong that was. How I've been keeping that from myself. But I don't feel any sense of relief, and it hasn't freed me of the depression – that still drifts in and out as it pleases.

When I was younger I would struggle when first emerging from a few dark days. There was always a slight sense of shame, a sort of reawakened self-awareness, an emboldened critic casting harsh judgements on everything that had just happened. Now there are grief and guilt too.

This was one of the first things I learnt as I began to find out how to live with this voice inside me: the spirals. The ever-tightening concentric lines, turning in and in on themselves, tightening until they form a perfect circle. A dot that disappears. A nothing at the centre.

The real devil is how you criticise yourself for feeling bad, declare yourself a failure, then criticise yourself for feeling worse, then repeat and repeat and repeat. Criticise is a weak word here. It doesn't carry the weight required of it. Hate isn't even quite enough. Sometimes the violence is beyond language. It is an inferno, created by you and turned in on yourself. Fire fuelled by fire.

The layers and layers of thinking this can create are hard to understand, even if you've experienced it a great deal. It can be difficult to see that anything is happening, that there is something moving deep inside you, that this is a process, an experience that can be put into words, explained and contained. But what is perhaps most frightening of all is that, over time, you get incredibly good at this. You are, after all, relentlessly practising a skill, a reaction to a situation, a response to a stimulus.

The colours of life start fading around you, and you panic. You do, however, know what you're going to do next because you've done this before, and you always do the same. You have spent years perfecting ways to destroy yourself. To be kind isn't possible, but also isn't really impossible. That would suggest an idea formed from other ideas, like horses with wings or people breathing underwater, but to call for kindness is to plead with a black hole.

What came so much later was how to know the voice was speaking without always listening to it. Sometimes that doesn't work, and at its most devious you don't even know there's anything to listen to. It slowly takes hold of you and ever so gradually turns off the lights, sometimes over hours, sometimes over days. It is an endless rising pressure, a pain that can only increase.

158

But, with help and support and a thousand false starts, you will slowly, slowly, slowly learn how to stop listening. How to break a spiral as it begins. Even how to recognise it before the spinning has started.

I try to remember this in these times. To be kind, to stop listening, to keep moving. To remember that failing doesn't make me a failure. I try, over and over and over.

I will go back to the cottage later, I will, to see what is left. To see where I can go from here. But this time I will bring kindness to myself and the situation. I will try to forgive myself, fractionally, eventually. To forgive Dad, even, for my absence from his notes. Maybe I was everywhere already and didn't need to be mentioned. Maybe.

I am here now. Stuck in guilt and confusion, in all of our words and all of our silences. I need to find something, make something of this moment.

I will go back to the cottage, to look again. I will.

Two trips out today, early morning, late afternoon.

The first was methodical, surveying the trees nearby, looking for the smallest clues and changes. But nothing. All was as before, as a hundred times before.

Later was different. I wanted to move more quickly, to run and feel the wind dancing around me. I warmed up around the cottage, on the flat ground. Stepping lightly, building the pace as my breath quickened.

Then out and up. Not too far past the forest, but looking for changes in rhythm, rolling ground that balances up and down, not the sheer effort of climbing then falling. This might be the most enjoyable running of all, with each burst of uphill effort instantly rewarded by a short rush down again. Push, then glide.

I stopped after a while, having travelled much further than I'd intended. I was smiling. Simply and easily smiling. A moment to quietly hold on to.

Then the trip back, slower now with tired legs, but satisfying still. Back along the rolling, early slopes, back to the point where I usually leave and enter the forest.

But something had shifted in the world around, a darkness lifting over the treetops.

Something had shifted in me.

9.31am. Cool. 3.26pm. Cool.

I like this note very much, and have been desperately trying to find anything that matches it.

I want to know what he saw that day, or how he saw it. He feels positive, in control here. No devil standing over him, not even Mum casting her beautiful shadow.

It feels like a small moment of closure, or acceptance. Not a beginning necessarily, not a straight and even road, but a glimpse of life after her death. Of holding on to things that they loved, that he could still love alone.

160

There are no clues, as every page is still anonymous, undated, unknowable. The same paper, same writing, no patterns that tie anything together.

This note gives me hope. Something shifted for him. I just can't find what it was, or where it led him. I can't find the page that comes next.

SHIFTED

SHIFTING

SHUFFLING

PAPERS NO MORE

Today was in the light. I am taking nothing for granted. Trying to think of what is and can be, not what I see, what can be seen.

What is hidden? What else is there, beyond this moment, beyond my limits of perception and imagination?

I sat for a long time, on a rounded peak, a lower one, feeling the sun move around the glen. Watching it stir the water below. Mirroring, bright, burning, dark. Watching it push my shadow around me, over the rough grass and smoothed stones. Watching how the earth shifts underneath it all.

Then clouds that come and go, rain that washes in, misting, drizzling, hard spitting, then gone. Listening to the wind move, softly calling. Whispering, then roaring.

Each moment is made of so much. Nothing stays still, nothing stays the same.

I still have so far to go to find her.

She is an echo, a shadow. She is fading.

6.47pm. Cold.

I see what he means, about Mum's shadow. I see it everywhere, feel it everywhere, but it is still distant and unclear.

At the cottage, standing in the doorway, out on the slopes, up on the peaks. It gets cast in different ways on different days.

Today it was the sound of birdsong, taking me back to the cremation, to that feeling of death, being small and defeated, shrouded when you've lost someone. That day I learnt birdsong could be both beautiful and tormenting, able to draw me away from myself, away from the worries of the world, but also to sting, to burn, to hurt.

Her shadow is everywhere, and everywhere it is painful. I watch the sun sink lower.

CALLING

CALLING

FALLING

NOW

That's one of many parts of this that are so challenging: he was there that day. We scattered her ashes together. She was given to the earth and the wind hundreds of miles from the Highlands, and yet he is here, was here, looking for her in gaps and cracks, between beams of light. If that even makes any sense.

They were here together, he was here alone. Both are true, but true at such a distance that it barely matters. I try and place them inside the cottage, cooking, eating, smiling, holding each other, but it is so painful to picture. I am staring right into the sun and can see nothing. I come back to it again and again, but still it burns.

I am angry with him and feel sorry for him. I want to scratch and fight and swear, but also want to hold him, reassure him, say sorry, sorry, sorry, then talk him down from this edge.

At this point it is all edges.

SLIP

TRIP

FALL

EDGE OVER EDGE

FALLING

FALLING

FALLING

Today was a chase. I felt uncomfortable from the start, distracted, uncertain. I slept badly last night, even worse than normal, then woke roughly.

I decided to get out, but get out slowly. I can't risk being hurt, then falling further behind her. The Devil has my attention, it is reaching out to me. Circling.

Walking, not running. Walking, not climbing. To be safe, as safe as I can be. The weather was still, but I was startled, jumping at the slightest rustle, creak, or crack as the trees leant against each other, steady but wrestling.

Past the forest edge, walking on. A little lighter, a little less noise in my head. Looking out over the beautiful, wild ground spread before me. Remembering not to be distracted, not to be called away. Noticing but not getting carried away by it. I need to stay focused, to remember why I am here, who I am here for.

A little quicker, a little quicker. Maybe moving will help, but not fast, no risks, remember that I am being distracted. Remember, remember. I need to breathe and move, to feel blood flowing, to smooth some of the edges of anxiety away.

Following an old path, a former military road, wondering about all those who have passed along it, hikers today and soldiers before. A path cut into nature, through it, marking and scarring, invading and controlling, trying to dominate what has always been here. Changes that cannot be unchanged.

The path rolls through the hills. Steps cut into the ground, giant flagstones and loose gravel, with hard rock seams rising from the ground beneath, cutting against the smoothed surface. The path is flanked on either side with coarse heathers, plants that will survive any storm or snowfall.

In the corner of my eye something moves, bouncing through the air. A tiny bird, too small and too quick, emerges from the long grass and swiftly disappears again. I can hear its musical call, thinking of her, how she would have known instantly what it was. Calling, again.

Just enough. Just enough distraction, a moment of lost focus, and my foot caught. Falling. Hurt. Lying spread over the path, bleeding into the dirt.

The Devil did this, I know it did. Using everything against me.

Nothing can be trusted. Nothing.

4.36pm. Blustery.

ALL AND ALL

WHISPER

WHISPER

READY TO BURN

I had furious dreams in the night. Neon red jackets were flocking over the mountains, high in the air, wheeling and screeching from above.

Winged waterproof creatures, twisting, flapping, mobbing each other. Lunging and pecking from beneath their hoods, fabric folded over a terrible lurking darkness.

Light catching the red, that neon red, that memory turned into a chasing cloud, shoaling, fighting against the wind, changing shape to fly, to attack.

Then all at once they saw me, turning again, coming towards me with all their heat and neon red speed. Until they hit.

I woke in shock and darkness, and could think of nothing but crows flocking over carrion, taking flesh that no longer has any other use.

Have I been trying enough, or too much?

Regardless, time is slowing and weather is passing quickly. The clouds are being blown away. They too are lost, over and over.

Day after day I have resolved myself, drawn upon my failure. Returned, rested, dried everything out. Stretched, slept, cried. Silently sat in the deepest centre of a cold woodland that cares neither for me nor the life and death between its roots and branches.

I have seen everything. Every bit of the forest, every mountain edge, peak, and hollow. In sunlight, in rain, some snow, all of the wind. I have looked for the gaps between scattered shards of sunlight, waiting for clouds to shift and part, open and reveal. But I have missed something. I have missed me.

There is place, there is light and weather, but there is a person too. So far I have not tested myself enough. I am getting in the way of finding her.

I need to find my edges, and step beyond them. Coldly and with confidence. Beyond all exhaustion. There she lies, alone and afraid.

I can rescue her, I can. I simply have to give more.

Morning. Early. Frost.

There are a few of these, which I didn't spot at first. Something feels more worrying about them. The tone has suddenly changed, beyond the grief he was already feeling.

It is dark, but it doesn't feel like despair. It is something else. It is his commitment to her now realised, now complete. His commitment to finding her and bringing her back.

You can almost hear his own devils, talking between the lines. You can almost hear the fight.

I am a few days into another set of experiments, another start, stop, fail, start.

I am tired, which is the point. I have run further, I have slept less, I have embraced every edge I can find.

Nearer now to something new and different, but carefully. There is danger here. I am close to somewhere, something. Closer to her, but still not close enough.

There is pain, muscles and joints, scraped elbows and knees, my body's frayed edges. But that is a small, small price.

I must go on.

Afternoon, nearly evening. Darkening.

167

4.

This is it. I've found it. Not single-sided, not double-sided, but instead a map folded over and over itself. I'm not sure how I missed it before, but it's so tiny it could easily have been wedged between other pages, hidden during the rush of sorting and stacking, as I was stuffing all of Dad's wild thoughts away into cardboard boxes.

It is an intricate map, painstakingly put together, with far more detail than any of the other sketches. It almost looks like it was created by a different person, but it's definitely his writing. And, again, a single word at the centre of the page.

Hotel.

That other sketch, the page that caused me so much frustration, was vague and out of focus. This one is sharp, clear. There are points here I can recognise, can connect to. The cottage is marked, and the river. I can start with this, I can follow it. Now I have somewhere to start from.

There are pages to distract and pages to look for. Some lead towards, some lead away.

I hope the Devil is reading this.

I can hide too.

I can be in control too.

Morning. Bright.

His map doesn't quite match the other ones I've collected – it has more detail, and less. Several outlined shapes that could be buildings or rock formations don't seem to be on the official maps, while several key details in the Ordnance Survey maps are missed off his, or edited out. His is a clean, sharp collection of what he needs to know and no more.

So, if I'm following it correctly, I'm heading up the main slope then turning away from the path to Dad's first encounter with his hallucinated devil, heading in the opposite direction, leaving the hollow behind. Away from that hole in the ground, that steep-sided pit of despair. I can't, won't go back to it. His pain is sharpest there, hardest to ignore there.

To the west instead, following the ridge after a series of false peaks, along an incredibly rough, rocky route, then to a cluster of trees that sits behind the summit I've spent all these weeks looking up at. Beyond are the beginnings of another vast forest, other glens that branch out from the same mountain.

Why this is important I do not know, but it is. It's something. Not quite a clue, I can't think that, can't get ahead of myself. Remembering that neon red jacket, remembering those notes from nowhere. Remembering all the conclusions I've jumped to. But Mum and Dad went to that hotel, they definitely did. It meant something to him, means something to him, something unsettling. A place he might have returned to.

It is a path to be followed, at the very least. A new direction to go in, after tracing twisted circles for so long.

Follow and follow. Sometimes all we can do is follow. Follow a path, a hope, something seen from far away.

Follow until you can find. Until you find somewhere to start from, to lead from.

I will follow, then I will find, then I will lead.

Morning. Clouding.

It's a tough trip, or seems like it will be, so I'm preparing properly. Climbing that high could be dangerous if the weather turns, if the clouds come in and visibility is lost. It looks clear out now, but you never know how things will look in a few hours when you're that far up, when the temperature drops and everything changes.

Hiking boots, a bag, food, water, compass, a safety whistle, extra layers, a space blanket, my maps, and his map. I have to be ready.

I am nervous, horribly nervous, but I have focus. For the first time in too long I know what I should be doing, what I need to do. I have a clear route.

Starting is simple, for once. Out of the cottage and through the forest, not a chalk mark to be seen, the ground soft and springy after a long dry spell. Too long for this time of year. Another thing that has changed. I'm warming a little from moving quickly, with purpose, watching light bleeding in as the horizon of trees untangles itself, as gaps emerge that weren't there before. Then out, past the big rock, to the slope, and up.

Moving up and away from the hollow, away from that terrible, confusing note that has cast so much doubt and despair, the first time he saw his devil. Knowing that he is ill, was ill, as I am, as I have been. Knowing too that illness can be recovered from, if only you can see it, if only you can understand that it is happening. I need to see what is really happening to me.

Now it gets tough. The mountain sharpens and sharpens, finally peaking not in a single point but a jagged ridge that runs for a mile or more. A knife blade made of rock. To either side the view is overwhelming, stretching for many miles over wild and ranging forests, over lochs and tiny lochans. I see waterfalls roaring silently at this distance.

Taking a breath, I look down, knowing I have to watch my steps to keep safety within grasp. This is truly dangerous. Crouching over, I grab on to rocks, finding cracks for my fingers, testing footholds before I take them. I may be no expert in reading maps, but even I understand enough to have stayed away from here until today.

171

Is there another way to the hotel? Perhaps, but not according to Dad's map. This is the route he traced, one of the details he chose to include. This is part of his edit, his way of looking at this mountain, breaking an ancient monument into fragments.

Keep going, keep going. Wiping sweating palms against my trousers, trying to keep friction, friction that helps me cling on. Looking for any hint of shining rock, any moisture that could send a foot sliding away. Looking at hands, then feet, then hands, then feet. Seeing only the narrow gap of safety to navigate, crushed on both sides by a sheer drop.

Eventually the ridge softens, widens, begins to resemble something closer to a path. The scrambling eases into careful walking and I can allow myself time to stop and properly look, to compare what is in front of me with the map I was left.

I can see the forest edge, but no hotel. I skip a beat but tell myself this is fine, that so much can be hidden by these huge trees. I may not be looking in the right direction, it may all have become overgrown in the decades since they were last here, since it was a working hotel. Didn't he mention something like that, of the forest taking everything back, of reclaiming? That makes sense, I think, I make myself think. I try not to get carried away, try not to imagine how this could end, might end, should end.

Remember that neon red jacket. Remember not to trust what you hope for.

The air is cooling slightly. Not cold, though, not too cold for being this high on a mountain, completely open and exposed. It is still dry,

172

thankfully. That ridge would be death in the rain. Simple and unavoidable death, day or night. I take a breath, remember to breathe, in and out, to try and calm the panic as it rises.

Neon red jacket, neon red jacket, neon red jacket.

A story is starting somewhere deep inside me, that hard, quiet voice again. I know it is whispering, but I try not to listen. To be aware of it without hearing it, without letting it sink in. I know this and can do this. I can, I can, I can.

Come back to now. Focus. The map, check the map. Dad's tiny, precise lines seem to follow the mountain as it tumbles and spreads down into this other forest. There's what I think is a river marked and, looking up, I can see water shining between some of the trees. Taking points of reference from the map and the land, trying to bring them all together in calm clarity.

I catch myself slowing down and realise how hard I've pushed to this point. It's already been two or three hours and I am exhausted. I have hiked and climbed and scrambled flat-out, working harder over the ridge than I should have, risking more than was really necessary. I am grinding on towards this mark on a piece of paper, pushing myself because I have so little left. Because all I have is the hope that it will lead me to something, anything.

But what to find? Again, stories, stories, stories. Jumping to the end of something that hasn't even started. Stop it. Please stop it. It's starting, I can hear it, I know I can. Be aware, but don't listen. Please don't listen.

Get moving, I tell myself. Keep moving. Pull the breath back, know that will help, it always helps.

I am leading and I am here.

I can see everything from up here. I can see where they are.

I am coming, I am coming.

Afternoon. Wind lifting.

A little calmer now, nearing the forest edge, holding back my anger and anticipation. Will this be the end? But remember the neon red jacket, remember that terrible moment of thinking I'd found him, that story that ran ahead, that escaped. That time he had the wrong face.

I still can't see any signs of a hotel, of anything but cold, hostile wilderness. I stop and check and re-check the map, but it's no good. It all makes sense. Everything connects. The detail, for once, is precise and accurate. It is showing me where to go after so long swirling in uncertainty. I need to keep going and keep going, as I have through all these weeks and months.

I kept going at the crematorium, as we held each other, then when he left, with the police back home, in the attic, on the road, winding through these forests, to the abandoned, crumbling cottage, to more police up here, to paper and paper and paper. I found so much and yet there is nothing.

Keep going. I am down from the mountain now and walking into these new trees, crossing another line, finding my way again. It should be easier to see here as there is a long, thick stretch of larch trees, their needles browned and dried, fallen to the ground. Bare and no longer blocking the view. A rustling carpet of burnt orange.

Check the map again. This still looks like the right way, but I've found nothing yet. I keep turning around, making sure I can see the mountain path, see the way back out. To keep some sort of anchor for myself, a point to return to. But this isn't working, at least not here. Time to move further into the forest, to move across, to spread out.

But no hotel. Nothing but trees and trees, a wall of Scots pine behind the bright larch. This happens sometimes. It's all normal, it could be normal. Tell yourself that. Remember the safe thing to do is to retrace, pull back, find your way to try again. Remember doing this with Mum and Dad, trying to calmly hold a moment of confusion as you turn and walk back the way you came, unpicking your steps until you can see clearly, until you can see your mistakes. Until you can start again.

So, I turn around and walk back out. Back through the larch, the shock of colour on a greying afternoon. I can really feel the cold now, which isn't helped by slowing down, by stopping to try and understand where I am. I can see my breath. I climb back up the slope a little to check the map again, to check his drawing, so detailed and yet totally insufficient. I can see the river, the forest edge, but what sits beyond? What did he line up to guide him?

Another peak, far beyond, is marked. That's the point where this forest fades out, struggling to cling on to another incline. That gives a line of three dots on the map, from the mountain path I came from, to the hotel, to that further peak. I was being pulled to the west when I should have been heading north.

I had been looking the wrong way. I let the lean and pull of the slope lead me down, my eyes drawn by the shock of deciduous autumn colour in an evergreen sea.

Back into the forest, this time keeping my sights fixed on that faraway peak ahead, not allowing my path to curve away from what I want more than anything, from what I am trying to find. From who I am trying to find. He must be. Surely.

But I can't think that.

This is it. Now is answers and waiting and patience and love, and anger and questions and all of the pain I have faced alone. She died. She died and he ran away. Never mind my words, what I said, he abandoned me when I needed him most. He left me alone so he could chase a shadow. He left me.

Deeper into the forest. This route is tough, thick with sharp branches that swipe at my arms and face, so it must lead to the side or back of the hotel. There must be a road up to the entrance, or perhaps there was long ago. Dad said something about views, about the hotel sitting above the land around it, towering over nature. There must be another way, but for now this is my way.

The forest is thick here and my head is ringing. It is a storm of half-thoughts and violent emotions. It is all this time alone, with no one to speak to, no one to share this pain and confusion with. And I need to try and stay centred, to stay in this moment instead of the one that is to come. Whatever that is. Stay in now. Breathe and breathe.

The trees are pressing closer and closer. Is this the way? I can no longer see the path behind or the peak far ahead. This is how maps fail, how forests can mislead, as everything merges into everything else. Stop. I mark a line on the ground directly in front and directly behind me, scuffing my foot into the mud to create a compass point. A straight line that connects the path behind to the hidden peak ahead, that should connect, that should meet the hotel somewhere in between.

This is surely it, if only I could find it. Stop, look around. Every direction looks the same. It is all dense trees, dark under the swaying canopy, darker now that the day is stretching on. I still need to get back before nightfall, but I know I have to keep going. Reaching the end is more important than getting back. Getting to the end is everything.

Take a breath, calm the stories, calm the spinning. Stop the noise. Follow the foot-scratched line in the mud. Walk straight, don't be blown off course, keep going and keep going. Is this the end? No, no stories, no more. It will be the arrival, whatever I find. Whoever I find.

The trees seem to thin out ahead, a patch of light coming through. Don't get carried away. Stop, mark the ground, look around. That's the only patch where anything looks different. This forest is unbelievably dense. Solid. Keeping in and keeping out. Follow the light, watch the trees detach from each other, gaps starting to form, more light coming through. The sound of the forest is changing, opening.

It is definitely a clearing, an artificial one, cut into the forest. Could this be it? I'm moving faster now, ignoring my tired legs and swollen feet, the heat and tension of blistering skin. Is this it? Moving on and on, running where I can, where the roots and ruts clear enough to allow more speed, to come closer and closer, until.

Until the trees end.

There is a hotel.

There was a hotel.

Now there is rubble, a grand old building that has been partly demolished. The front wall still stands, and the side walls, but it is hollow. The back of the building has been destroyed, revealing its skeleton. Again, I sit.

I sat in the crematorium. I sat in the attic. I sat in the cottage when I found the paper, and when I found those impossible notes later. I am always behind, I am always arriving after what is happening has already happened. Everything is in the past and I am nowhere.

There is no one here. No one. Those noises, those spinning stories of finding an ending, of what I would say to him, collapse into silence. There is a pause. I am holding my breath, tensing and tensing.

This must have been a beautiful location for a hotel once. There are huge, sweeping views from a grand arched entrance and paved terrace, though the glen this looks over is today flooded with cloud. It is hiding itself, ashamed. Besides the hollow hotel, there is nothing here but a small outbuilding that might have once housed serving staff or a groundskeeper. It is boarded up, locked, abandoned. It doesn't look like anyone has tried to break in.

And there is a road, of sorts, that would have led up to the hotel. There is a better way to get here, but it must lead far, far away from my cottage.

I check the map again and this is the location. I am doubting everything but certain of that. From here, freed from the hold of the forest, I can reconnect the mountain ridge I passed over to the other peak far away. The three dots are in a line again. The word on the map is correct. There is a hotel, there was a hotel.

But now it is not, and he is not. What is this? This cruel situation, these endless weeks of looking and never finding, of chasing something that has gone, someone who has gone. I know nothing and there is nothing to know.

Now only the hotel walls remain, only the walls you can see from the front, from the way you should arrive up the track. Perhaps it is going to be turned into something new, another hotel built inside the skin of the old one, reclaiming that invented heritage for other generations of wealthy people. For tourists and their luxury and escape.

I am finally ruined. I have lost him again. Chased, and lost. Seen, and lost. Invented, and lost.

I walk in a daze. There is nothing to see, no one to see, but still I look. I stumble over the rubble, see fragments of dark panelled wood, splintered now, and glass shards glinting in the dimming light. I walk in circles, still looking for him, still looking.

There is a hotel and no hotel. I have found and I am lost.

There is nothing here.

I am nothing.

She is still hidden. Completely hidden.

Afternoon. Darkening.

TURNING

TURNING

LOSING

LOST

5.

What comes next? I got back, somehow, through that forest and over that ridge, returning to the cottage as darkness was threatening. I must have managed to scramble the ridge, but I dare not think about that, about the risks I'd take to find someone who can't be found. I am, again, my Dad.

And I drove back to the rented house, slowly, in darkness. In the forest's darkness, the sky's darkness, and my own. Totally deflated, having been caught in an idea, in a promise, in the potential that this was it. That finally I'd found the clue, the secret, finally I'd found him.

What now is left?

SHIFTING

SHIFTING

LISTEN

NOW

This morning I went straight back into the forest. I couldn't stop, I can't stop.

A very intense memory from childhood came hurrying back to me. It is an odd, troubling memory and not one I've recalled for a long time. It felt surprising when it returned, cold and unwelcome.

I don't know why I would remember this, but I can't be sure of anything now. I don't know and am struggling to care.

It was a school race, cross-country, in the middle of winter. Ground frozen hard, rutted and crunching. Air fogged with hard breathing. A cloud of pre-teen misery, hundreds of footsteps that rumble through, then are gone.

Over the football pitch, crossing the edge of the playground briefly, then cinder track, local rugby club, car park, into woodland, a riverside path, wooden steps, a stretch of muddy trail arched with trees, then winding back down a hill to return through rugby club, cinder track, playground edge, football pitch, end. Running spikes scraping on concrete, the hard clat-clatting of football boots, all grinding through me.

For a handful there were team places to be won to race against other schools, while for most of us it would be a pointless trudge.

At this point I was new to running. I was starting to enjoy it, though a great deal still felt uncertain. I wasn't bad at it, but also wasn't good enough to be noticed and encouraged, coached and celebrated. On the edges perhaps, but not quite there.

And I was still trying to work it all out. There were others who were made from sport, who you felt might disappear without it. Classmates who had shining moments in front of others, for whom competition was something to be defined by.

I could see the draw of being challenged, but the fine line between winning and disappointment felt harsh and unnecessary to me. I wanted to battle myself, not beat others.

But in moments I was drawn in. That thrill would start to take hold. A whole other momentum gathering, beyond my body and its movements. Something it would take me many, many years to understand.

I'd sense my ability, at least relative to those around me, and jump headlong into a shapeless story of future glory, of soon being noticed, adored. A champion, declared by all.

Some stories have claws. They don't let go easily. Sometimes these writhing, fantastical monsters grow in you slowly, but sometimes they're born fully formed, adult, already hooked deep into your flesh. Confusing the line where it ends and you begin, drawing you from the what and the why.

Something too that changes, shifts, steps further away whenever you get close.

I didn't want to race, but I did want to run. And as we stretched out on our winding course, I began to realise that I was closer to the front than I'd thought. Not close, but closer. Cresting the top of the final hill everyone ahead was on display, with the leader almost in reach.

And a story started telling itself, a beast began to grow. Perhaps today I would call it a devil.

The story was of pushing on, a surprise, a minor triumph, a spot on the school team. There was no medal, no trophy, just a spinning that started and could not be stopped.

I gritted my teeth and willed everything. The clamour within me built and built. In moments I almost embraced the all-consuming pain, felt joy in it, while always, always wanting it to stop. But I didn't stop. I couldn't.

My mind was racing too – how many spaces, who's that in front, can I catch one, two, three, more? Do I push on now and risk, or hold back and risk? What more do I have to give? What more am I?

And the end of the memory blurs, scraping feet over concrete again, nearly falling but not quite, on to the grass, then it all stops. I don't remember much of the wider picture, but a few specifics are bright and brilliant.

There was cheering, and some of it was for me. Some classmates who'd already finished, some teachers exchanging amazed looks as I hurtled towards the finish line. I'd pushed everything, reaching for the edge of myself, just as Dad did all these years later.

Then congratulations, delight, warm words from a kindly older teacher. But the words didn't quite fit. They didn't match my story. The beast, claws still firm in flesh, stretched and bristled. A low, rumbling growl.

You made the squad! Runner-up. A back-up place, an option.

I might have been one place off making the team, or even two or three. It didn't matter, because it didn't fit the story. The whirling tale of victory that had emerged from nowhere, taken my body and rushed away with it, was broken.

And then another story begins. The claws aren't as obvious this time. They are thinner, but longer. They reach much further, much deeper into you, into the you of you, but might not be noticed at all. Even, or ever.

You failed, so you are a failure. You tried, but it wasn't enough. It will never be enough. The cheering wasn't gleeful, supportive, but mocking. They're laughing at you for thinking you could achieve it, achieve anything. You imagined success, being a success, but then failed all the same.

I cried over that. Over something I didn't want until moments before I lost it.

There can't be a devil chasing Dad around the mountains, a devil chasing me and keeping us apart, but there is still this story. That is my devil, and he may well have his own, have had his own, that I never knew about.

Stories can be beautiful ways to understand the world around us, but these are something else entirely. The word doesn't fit. They are an overwhelming aggression, planned and enacted against yourself.

Distraction and erosion, until you are broken into unrecognisable pieces.

Until the hotel is demolished and everything is rubble.

Close, close, close.

I am near to something, but it is fleeting.

I must be quick. All of the edges are coming together. Something is opening, revealing, waiting. Something will happen.

I am always tired now, always in pain.

Always chasing and pushing.

But now I know I am close. Close to her.

Morning. Light rain. Bright.

MOVE

MOVE

MOVE

SPINNING

ON AND ON

I am close, I know I am, but something is wrong.

I need to keep pushing, but the tiredness is thick and heavy.

Ankle turned today.

Sharp pain from shoulder to elbow, from a slip, another slip.

Thought I almost fell asleep on the trail. Stumbling.

I am not in control now. I have to let go.

Afternoon. Clouds, hiding fierce sunshine.

MOVING

MOVING

TELLING YOURSELF NOW

MOVE

MOVE

MOVE

The Devil is here. This is it.

I have tried every edge but one.

Now is time for darkness, for the night.

Now I have to go, to rescue her.

Evening. Clouds parting. Moon waking.

STEP

STEP

MOVE

MOVE

LISTEN

LOSE

6.

The sun is fading now and I am still out, high on a peak. The light is a lure, a bright bundle of feathers dancing on the water's surface, baiting and enticing. That sounds like the sort of thing Dad would write. Maybe, maybe not, or not before he came here anyway.

When was the hotel? Two days, three days ago? It has all blurred together now.

I want to stay sat on the mountaintop, watching the sun slip below the horizon, feeling the last of the day's heat disappear. The effortless glide from fiery orange and dirty purple, to fading yellow and heavy navy, to dark. As colour too gives up, retreats, hides again. I could stay here forever. I have nowhere else to be.

But the longer I sit, the more risky the trip back down the mountain becomes. The greater the danger of a slip or trip, of rolling over an edge or tumbling down a steep slope. And other dangers too.

Dad always had a terrible fear of the night, so it's particularly hard to read the few notes where he's pushing on into the darkness, goading himself, risking everything to reach a state of spiritual exhaustion. His last move, the last thing he could attempt to try and find her, to bring her back.

Those notes read more like they were written by a member of a cult than someone lost, lonely, and grieving. But he was not corralled and converted, just desperately sad and sick. He was alone when he wrote these, regardless of what or where or whether he is now.

I pick myself up, take a deep breath, and slowly move down while I still can.

Light tames the wilderness, holding it back, however briefly. Night is its playground.

I must accept this. This is where she is. She is hidden in darkness, not to be found elsewhere.

I am close to ready.

I have prepared. Tracked slope and peak, worked through every inch of every forest.

I have looked into the light, the rain, the wind, the snow.

And now I have found my edges. Pushed on and on and on. Slept less, ate less, moved more.

I am light. I am clear.

It is now.

Now I have to go, to rescue her.

Nearly night. Cold, rain passed, wind picking up.

MOVING MOVING

BREATHING BREATHING

WATCHING WATCHING

WAITING

That dream again, that terrible dream. The neon red winged devils have been flapping and screeching all night.

I am lying, dead or injured, watching them peck viciously at me, fighting with each other, claws and beaks felt but not seen. Twisting fabric, pointing, pointing, pointing.

It is all heat and noise and loud, loud, loud, until it becomes unbearable. Until it stops. Until I return to darkness. To nothing.

Silent, in the darkness, but knowing everything that has already happened, everything that could happen again.

I am taking steps into the night now, feeling its difference, starting to adjust, to see the shades within the darkness.

Trying to be closer to it, to embrace, to find, to feel it.

190

And it's not just the same places without the light. It is something else, somewhere else. Transported and transformed.

I must transform too.

Nearer and nearer.

Now I have to go, to rescue her.

Night. Darkening. Beginning.

7.

I lit a fire today, in the cottage, for the first time. Maybe I was wrong to worry about feeling settled here, allowing myself a little comfort. Winter is chasing fast, but it's dry for now. The wind rips through.

I should move, so I can feel a little more alive than this. Get away from the cottage, from all the time I've spent here. Its gravity gets stronger as the weeks pass, as everything outside shifts and fades. The fire casts tiny flickering shadows on the walls, the only other movement there's been inside here since I arrived. I watch the flames and think of the bright blue fireplace in what used to be their home.

I'm being pulled under. I need to get out, to find the silence that only comes in motion, that special hidden feeling that is so slight as to be nearly impossible to find. It hides when you look, alert, shrinking into the undergrowth, arriving when you settle, when you stop hunting it.

Before I would chase so hard for some sort of peace, never understanding how foolish this was. Fighting for calmness, tensing to find relaxation, which of course can never work. Looking for ease in a teeth-clenched sprint.

And in that fight there is a moment that repeats, as your watch ticks down to the next big effort up a hill, or around a looping path, or from lamp-post to lamp-post, wherever you may be. A sickening moment of self-doubt, when you know that pain is coming, entirely optional pain, and you feel that urge to stop, to rest instead of steeling yourself to go again.

But each and every time, you decide that you will not quit, that you do not quit. Knowing that this is only true if you see the opportunity to stop, to fall short, and resist its pull. Becoming yourself in tiny fractions, in moments of deciding not to listen to the voice inside that calls you away.

What can be wonderful is feeling your sense of control growing. What can be crushing is the incessant need to improve, casting every achievement as less than it can be, less than another, real or imagined.

Today the weather is unsettled, the wind pushing the clouds through at pace, shadows disfiguring the ground below, repeatedly hiding and revealing, cooling and warming and cooling.

I need to move. I need to push myself against the day, against the slopes. Endlessly freezing, endlessly thawing. Feeling how movement opens up the possibility of change, introduces the idea of it, even though change may never come. It is possible. It must be possible.

I will step out. The fire has died already anyway.

I am moving. Slowly, to feel what aches, to tenderly try out where my right knee has been complaining, my lower back seizing, my neck and shoulder knotting.

I am moving, and I know roughly where I am going. Today I'll explore a route I've enjoyed a few times now, or almost enjoyed. Tentatively trying to find some pleasure out here, so I can remember what that is. Trying to move on from everything I haven't found, from all the decisions I cannot make.

The route starts a few miles further away than my regular hikes, up a wooded path that winds east of the nearest peak to the cottage. Far away from that awful hollow, even further away from the hotel. It seems to be a way to reach somewhere else more important and is barely a route in itself. A rolling climb, less steep, less severe than the mountainsides, a rough track dancing between trees. Stones claw out of the ground, ready to catch a toe, to stub you, trip you, and bring you down.

Everything is dry, soft underfoot. I listen to the hushing sound of my feet, my breathing, the shiver of a breeze as it stirs the leaves overhead. The canopy sounds like water, stirred, rippling. Far above that a buzzard cries, its call bleak and shrill.

When I was young, very young, we went on holiday further north than here, somewhere really extreme and remote. One of those parts of Scotland where trees barely exist, found only in pockets where the rain and wind haven't cleared them away. We were driving, Mum was driving. I sat in the back staring out in wonder. Such space, such distances, such a contrast from everything I was used to. Happy, aimless chatter bubbled.

We turned a corner on a single-track road. There, sitting calmly on a tree stump, only a few metres away, was an adult golden eagle. Fully grown, the most severe stare you can imagine, beak sharp and accusing, bright claws flecked with dried blood. Mum stopped the car and we all sat, silent, not wanting to lose the moment, barely understanding the moment, finding no words that could usefully embrace what we saw. This creature of the sky, perched almost at our level, entirely untroubled by us. A small red hatchback car and a glorious winged killer.

It sat and we sat. Then a twitch of the head, something heard far away, and a mighty opening of its wings, heavy sweeps to catch the air, to turn and glide, to disappear with no sound at all. We sat, stunned, long after it had gone. Dad muttered in disbelief, barely forming words. Mum said nothing, but turned to me with a smile of pure sunshine. That smile shared something so complex and personal that explaining it could only ever fall short. Falling short as these words are now.

I am making ground quicker now on the trail, feeling more comfortable, any imagined aches and anxieties eased and forgotten. I am starting to lose myself in the forest, far below the treetops. Here I am small and will be gone soon. Here I can forget. Here I can disappear.

A buzzard's cry again, nearer this time. They are everywhere here, mewing and calling, floating around each other. They are often mistaken for golden eagles by visitors to these mountains, looking for a piece of Scotland to take away with them, a memory they'd hoped to make. The difference between the two, however, is startling. The eagle's outspread wings are twice the size, with a presence that darkly menaces.

195

Mum often said that buzzards sound sad, that their cry is one of loss, mournful and raw. She loved these birds, their brown and white feathers, lazily wheeling around each other, lifted on rising air currents. She loved that they build their nests together, the male and female, and that in the air they seem to have nowhere to go, no rush, just floating on and on.

I'm quite far into the trail now and tiring slightly. Feeling hot despite the cold day, salt crusting on my lips and face. That sound again, that cry again. It's nearer. Sharper, louder.

Then feathered shriek, bursting from branches, tumbling out of the air.

Not gliding, but swooping, attacking. No longer up there, small, distant, beautiful, but here, dramatically here. Speeding towards me, moving so much faster than I can move. We face each other, quickly, briefly.

It swoops. I flinch and cower. The wings adjust just before it hits, pulling up, swerving between the trees and away. To return? It's crying again, the cat-like noise turned into a snarl.

Again it swoops, force and evolution and instinct focused into tiny claw tips, points sharpened to rip flesh, tear animals apart, alive or dead. Talons to shred, a beak to feed its young.

A nest? I must be disturbing it, scaring it into protecting its young. I am running fast now, elbows powering back, cutting their own lines through the air, knees lifting, eyes darting from the ground to the sky, knowing I have to get away, can't fall, can't fall and defend myself with bare hands and arms. Looking down and looking up.

But towards or away? Am I running nearer, making this worse, angering this creature and encouraging it to greater fear and panic? I am panic, we are panicking, causing each other fear, reacting and reacting. Blood pumping, coarse, heavy, hard. Breath and blood and fast, fast, fast.

Keep moving, keep moving, but steady, not so fast that this will suddenly stop, that oxygen isn't enough. A violent cry calls out behind, a little further away. Am I going the right way? Just keep going, keep focused, breathe and step and don't fall. Crying, closing in. It is coming again.

I spot the shadow over the dirt path before I see it, before it swoops. Suddenly dropping, all its weight given to gravity, feeling it accelerate as I try to keep moving. Looking up and looking down.

Dropping, claws flayed, eyes fixed, beak opened.

Trying to move and duck and keep moving.

Then wings spread, braking on air, it twists and rushes straight over my head, striking the air between us. Calling out its despair and mine.

I have to go. I am going. Faster, it has to be faster. Get through this and away, find another way, a way out, and never return. Get back to admiring these birds from distance, them in the air while I am rooted in the ground below. Running and ragged breathing.

It is higher now, the trail giving way to rocks, rough steps that I must climb, losing rhythm, losing speed. Hands on knees, pushing up and away, slowing and starting again, starting, no rhythm, no rhythm.

It is crying out, but further away now, and softer. Is it softer? I want it to be, I hope it is. I can't keep going much longer. Hard gasping, hard, hard. Slipping on rocks, thighs burning from pushing up and up.

Another cry, quiet, far. I stop and lean against a tree, bent over, no breath, no words. Nothing but breathing and breathing and waiting for this to pass, waiting for my heart to slow, just a little, waiting for my body's panic to settle.

Darkness, darkness calling. I know this is next, I know this is where she is.

This is where the Devil hid her, the only place I never looked, never could look.

Now I have to go.

Night. Darker.

The rasping has passed, the breath returned. I am walking now, hurting and walking, keeping on although the easiest route to the cottage would be back the way I came, through the forest. No, not the easiest, but the most direct. Now I am continuing up the slope, to find another path, to find another way back.

Protecting its young, it must have been. Fighting off a predator, a threat, someone who was coming to kill.

Would it really have attacked? Would it have sprung claws on me, into me, to draw blood and maim, or was the noise only to scare? Was the speed and suddenness, the shock, enough of an attack? I don't want to know.

From fast to slow. I'm tired now, shivering and sore, but have miles and miles to go. I need to think about a speed that I can manage for an hour or two. I need to find a rhythm that can last.

I love her, I will find her.

I am sorry for all this, so sorry. I can't describe my hurt and failure, that she is trapped, that I am not there with her, protecting her, beside her.

I love her, I will find her.

I will rescue her.

Night. Darker.

The walk has been steady, but tough. I am nearly back now. That sudden rush to escape has emptied me. My careful plan of ease and enjoyment suddenly torn up, left in pieces. Broken, again, as I break everything.

This is it now. I am here and deserve all that nature can throw at me. I have hurt and shouted and screamed and blamed. I have broken and deserve to be broken.

I'm finally back to the big rock, on the forest edge. It is cold now and the sun is falling. The wind is finding its voice.

Walking slowly through the forest, to my car, to leave. Or to leave as far as the house. Never getting too far, never getting far enough.

She is not hidden in sunlight, in light and clouds, she is hidden in darkness.

She is behind the only thing I cannot look at.

I am closer now, closer than ever.

I love her, I will find her.

I will rescue her.

Night. Darker.

I'm back at the car. Door opened, cold to the touch, inside, sitting. Sitting that could become sleep, but can't just yet. I think I will go back to the rented house. I think.

Legs tender, crying out with surprise as they reach for the pedals. Knowing that the pain tomorrow, or in a few days, will be so much worse. Tiny muscle tears aching with heat and stiffness, reluctant to flex and turn, to move in any ways that aren't timid, apologetic, meek.

I slowly drive back through the trees, down the long track to the main road, feeling the bumpy terrain eventually give way to the song of tarmac, its vibration and hum. Home soon.

No, not home. Tiredness, tiredness. Back to there, to rest and recover. To sleep.

But I wanted something else today.

I wanted to escape.

I wanted to feel alive.

SLEEP NOW

HEAVY HEAVY

LET IT FALL

DRIFTING

DRIFTING

SOFTLY

FALLING

8.

The night was awkward, uncomfortable, dreaming of being chased through train stations, a church, a supermarket, along a canal. All empty, with no sign of the chaser, nothing visible, just a certainty that I needed to flee. Not the mob of neon red jackets this time, but something else, something new. Curiously, all the locations were in a nameless city, a bit like home but with the streets cut up and rearranged, making new connections and new dead ends.

I wake in the rented house and get up slowly, carefully, knowing how the pain will shoot. Once this might have felt like a badge of honour, a pride in training furiously hard, pushing my limits further and further again, but not today. I made no choice to run that hard, for that long. I had no choice to stop. I don't want to imagine if I had stopped, what that might have been, how that could have ended.

Would the bird actually have attacked? I'm not sure, really not sure. I keep telling myself that would never happen, that it was just a warning to push me away from a nest site, away from what is most precious. The words I use are clear, the logic sensible, but emotionally I am detached. I don't believe that I was safe at any point until I got away, at any point before I got back here.

Today the rain is loud. That incredible, lashing rain you get here, that feels as if it could wash everything away. I am sitting, listening to it patterning the roof and windows. Being inside when it rains can feel calming and warm, or tense and claustrophobic. Today I am trapped.

Somewhere out there, that buzzard still sits in its nest. The path below is being washed, raindrops crashing from branch to branch, running down pine needles, pausing at each pointed end, clinging on until they fall to the next and the next.

Little rivers will be swelling on the tracks, flowing down wherever people or animals have smoothed a way, cutting into the hillside, rippling, deepening.

FLOODING

FLOODING

FLOODING

I am trying to stay on my feet, reminding myself that forcing blood to muscles is healing, that pain is a part of recovery, that stopping and sitting still isn't enough. Some resting, some movement, some balance is needed. Then pushing yourself gently, to find if there's further you can go, if your body can take it. Finding how far you have healed. Finding by hurting.

Where I am and why I'm here has all become faint and distant, detached and other. In moments I am watching myself, wondering about myself, thinking about thinking about finding.

Where are you, Dad? Why this? Can this not be something else? Can I not be somewhere else?

I have no choices. Everything has happened and I am still so far behind. Now I know less than ever. Now I know nothing.

You are dead. You are not dead. You fell from the spine of one of the highest ridges and your body is broken, cold, hidden in some crevice far from sight. You are still searching. You are with Mum. You are not with Mum. You are together and finding and searching and lost and scared and relieved and alone.

You are lost and I have not found you, have found nothing of you, but I have found something else. I have begun to.

I have found more of me, in all this madness, the start of some clarity in the pages, in the impossibilities, in the notes that follow notes, that create edges and turn corners, that ask so much and answer nothing.

I have found more, I am finding more, but indistinct, out of focus. I am moving towards being able to see myself but slowly, slowly, slowly. So slowly.

SLOW

SLOW

SLOWING

SLOW

SLOW

STOP

I will start. I really will.

I need to start.

NO STARTING

STOPPING

STOPPED

It's drier now, still raining but a faint glow is trying to escape the clouds. The worst of the stormy skies are moving off, up towards the highest ridge that sits between here and the real danger. Where the roads don't reach, where the roads don't even overlook, fenced in by peaks for miles and miles and miles.

I used to love that in wilderness you can see the weather before it happens. You can see it blowing towards you from great distances, watching the light change over the hills beyond, waiting for it to reach you. Watching clouds being pushed up a steep slope, rolling over themselves, being stretched and shaped. Seeing rain fall while you are still dry, smelling as it draws closer, arriving in cautious bursts and then all at once.

I used to love looking further, to a horizon that is far, far away, but now even that feels too close. Everything is so near that I can see nothing clearly. Now I don't want to look.

In this house, at the cottage, in the forest, on the hillside, at the peaks, I can see nothing. In the hollow where he first saw, thought he saw a devil, that awful space Dad wrote of and I shivered in, where his collapse began its freefall, I can see nothing.

Perhaps there is nothing to see.

I cannot see, I cannot be seen.

SEEING

WATCHING

WAITING

I'm still uncomfortable, but not so sore. I can go back to the cottage later.

It could be worse. No, not that. The pain could be worse from my aching muscles, swollen joints, and bruised flesh. The pain couldn't be worse of a dead parent, of dead parents, of all these confounding mysteries. I am playing a game without rules, grabbing in the dark at nothing, grabbing in the dark for a certainty, any certainty.

Even a body, another body, would be a certainty. I want that and don't want that.

I need something else. Should I leave? I need to leave, to be able to leave, but can't. I need something to leave for. I can't see anything, I can't see him, I can't see Mum either. I'm finding it hard to picture her, that beautiful face fading now, blond hair curling around a blur. Photos do nothing to fill this in, disappearing as soon as I look away. She is dead, but I am still finding new ways to lose her.

I know he's dead, but don't know he's dead. He knew Mum was dead, but didn't know. I was there, he was there. I know I'll never find anything in those notes, but still I read them. I know I'll never bump into him in the cottage, in the forest, up a mountain, but still I look. I keep looking, never, ever stopping.

I know and I don't know.

I know she is here, waiting, hidden, held.

I know her patience and strength, that she will be holding on, will still be there in this silence, still thinking of me.

I think of nothing else. I am nothing else.

Night. Darker.

And I am nowhere else, or nowhere here, not in these words and barely in these mountains. I am a haze, early morning mist to be burnt away by the rising sun. It might be time to disappear, if only I could, if only I was strong enough.

There must be another way through this, a better way of looking at this. I am too close, I am too far away.

I am too tired, drained by all my chasing and escaping, by Dad's continuous falling, down and down through his love and his words.

He was looking up, and never saw that the ground beneath him had disappeared.

I am nearly ready now, nearly ready.

I will rescue her.

Night. Darker.

9.

I have an idea, small, emerging, not quite formed enough to write down.

Something to hide and protect. Something that might help.

TOO QUICK

TOO CONFIDENT

QUIET VOICE

SLOW

STEADY

SLOW

STOP

He was obviously very unwell in those last few days or weeks of writing, which makes reading these pages extremely painful. It is

209

another kind of exhaustion altogether, and I frequently have to step away, regroup, walk through the forest slowly and collect myself before returning for more.

However, while I've been here in the Highlands a few different things have come together, a few quiet thoughts that I've had for a long time and never been quite able to pick out over the rest of the noise. Not bad quiet, that hard voice inside me, but for once good quiet.

Dad was experimenting with a dangerous sort of letting go, a total loss of control in the service of finding her, rescuing her, bringing her back. What I need to try, ever so gently, is a positive letting go. An empowerment in not trying any more, in ending the brutal, spinning stories, the breathlessness and rage, before it even begins.

Instead of chasing peaks and embracing difficulty, I need to look for slow and simple. Instead of timing, racing, measuring, and creating the potential for failure, I just need to move. Without judgement, without expectation, and crucially without any fiction that could explode and take me away with it.

A lot of this comes from bits of meditation I've tried over the years, coming back to a passing, vague interest Dad had in Buddhism, in a detached sort of spirituality. But it's also coming from what's happened since Mum's death, since Dad's disappearance, since their deaths that can't be but are. What good is chasing? Where has it got me?

It has helped, sometimes, that ability to grit my teeth and never stop, but it's also destroyed so much. And damaged me so much along the way. That I see clearly now. I am trying to accept that this process of improving, easing, letting go, whatever you might call it, will take years. It will take until the day I die, and still not be finished. But that doesn't matter. It will be its own challenge. Each step can be a reward.

No one is watching. No one cares. And that, perhaps more than anything, is completely freeing. It sounds bleak but might actually be wonderful.

Move, breathe, move. There is nothing else, really.

NO

QUIET VOICE

I AM YOU

LISTEN

LISTEN

LISTEN

Dad had it wrong. Over and over, step, step, step. Pushing forward, trying. Always trying, always moving on to the next thing.

My small idea feels uncomfortable, odd, misshapen. Out of place, and with no place.

The answer isn't to move, but to be still. Not step, step, step, but breathe.

Take the time to separate yourself, to find the spaces in between everything, the space between the shock and the reaction, the smallest moment between being pushed and falling.

It is time to find that gap, to hold it, and nurture it. To watch it quietly, without judgement or expectation, to let it grow without forcing it.

Breathe in, breathe out.

I have lost and grieved and need to finally move on from here.

It is time to silence these devils.

STUPID

STUPID

WORDS WILL NOT HELP

WORDS DO NOT STOP FIRES

I think it's been a few days. My head is buzzing again. I thought things were getting better, could get better, I thought I'd seen something new. I have, I know I have, but my breath is being pushed out again.

Everything is being pushed out. I eat, sometimes. Am I sleeping? Sometimes here, sometimes there. I light a fire in the cottage. I let my fears drift.

I'm trying to be calm, but know what I've done, what I've done to him. That I repeat and repeat, that I can't help myself. That I burn everything around me. That they are all dead.

Breathe. I've been here before, over and over. I know it will pass. Time to be kind, to hold on, to breathe in, breathe out.

Be kind, be kind, be kind. Don't let the darkness cloud. Even if it does, it will pass. The sky is still there, and it is still a glorious blue, hidden behind the grey.

I know I need to let go, but something inside me is holding on. Talons sunk in. Blood drawn.

So remember: I am not my thoughts. I am not the clouds. I am the sky, blocked, but still there. Unchanged, just obscured.

Breathe in, breathe out.

Forget those burning words. How I hurt him, pushed him away, forced him here.

There is always a gap between everything, between the trigger and response. There is always space for a breath. To stop, to pause the spinning. To stop and stop and stop.

Forget. Please, forget.

Remember, you are the sky, not the clouds. Please be kind. Don't be cruel for not being kind. Don't start spinning that circle again, that story.

Spinning all those things you have done, and why you are here, and why you deserve this and all of this.

Let everything go.

I am the sky, not the clouds.

They will pass, they always do. The wind will take them.

Still here, still here.

I hate, hate, hate this.

BURNING SOON

BURNING NOW

IT WILL COME

Panicking, feeling that familiar spin and circling, familiar not welcome, known not wanted, that tension that builds, clenching, feeling it start in my jaw, biting on nothing, muscles twitching and grabbing, then tensing in my legs, then quick thoughts, ever so quick, it is spinning, all spinning, quick grab breaths, not deep breaths, in, in, in, just hold, no exhale, no time for that, quick thoughts, grabbing at thoughts, ice in the throat now, quick breaths in, blocked by the ice, choking on the ice, a lump, held in the throat, want to be sick now, to breathe in now, to breathe out now, but blocked and blocked and blocked, blocked never to thaw, ice that cannot thaw, stuck, choking on a thought, jaw set now, teeth crushing teeth, to be crushed, to be split and ground and turned to dust, then jawbone holding jawbone, a grip that will never end, and sickness now, sick in my stomach, not butterflies but wolves with teeth and claws, turning, prowling, ready to tear out, I'm choking, choking, choking on the ice, but remember to breathe, feel the gap in between, but there is no gap, just breaths made of glass, broken glass, shards stuck in throat flesh, tiny glass needles, bleeding now, bleeding under the ice, glass and ice, all shards and shattered, lungs filling with blood, drowning in glass-sharded lung blood, and frozen, and quick thoughts, quick thoughts, spinning, spinning, feeling those talons sink in, the story sink in, this is me and me, this is the me of how I do and how I always do, this is me and I am this, I deserve this, I deserve the glass, the ice, the spinning and spinning, this cannot stop, please make this stop, this will never stop, spinning, sharded, surely bleeding, choking on the ice still, it will not thaw, feeling it, its coldness, quick breaths, all in, no out, this is panic, this can't be real, it is all real, this is the me of me and maybe now I die, I die too, I choke on throat ice, I drown in glass-sharded lung blood, this is real and always and now and stories and not stories and everything and the very me of me of who I am and all the everythings I have failed at and forgotten and missed and broken and all the ways I could never be and why this and why was I ever and

NOW AND HERE

LISTEN

YOU ARE HERE

HEAR ME

Dad, I have nothing left.

I know you are gone, but I don't know where. I will never know where.

You left notes and then left notes.

So much of everything made no sense, makes no sense.

I am here and must leave.

My words weigh heavy, heavy with their own darkness.

All is slow now, clouded.

I am the clouds.

The blue sky has gone.

The Devil is here.

Now I will step out for the last time.

Now I will find her.

I will bring her back.

Night. Dark.

Darkness

Burning. I can smell burning. The white light of terror. What is it?

I've fallen asleep in the cottage again, too immersed in the papers and the writing. Getting lost in the sea of words, rolling with the waves. Confused and disorientated, far from land.

It must be outside. I'm scraping myself out of sleep, slow and cold, rolling off his creaking camp bed, fully dressed inside my sleeping bag.

It is dark. What time is it? I don't think I've slept long – it's not morning, still evening. The day hasn't turned yet. That strange sensation of time being slippery, of not being where I left it.

Checking my watch, it's a little after 10pm. Winter is here now. These past few weeks it gets dark around 4pm, and it gets dark quickly. When the sun steps below the peak of the far mountain ridge the light is turned off, then everything is gone.

What would be burning outside? It's too late, too far from anything. It doesn't make sense. I'm probably imagining it. The cottage feels colder and more hollow than ever, each breath forming clouds.

But the smell is still there, forcing itself on me. It is burning of the harshest kind: not bonfire and comfort, but inferno and death. I look around, but see nothing. It is here and not here.

And I am suddenly far away, back in my teenage years. Left at home for a few days, trusted with the house while my parents took off for the mountains. Left alone, I think, for the first time. Possibly even so they could come here.

Moments turn. Calmness and peace are invisible things, ignored while you have them, craved when you don't. All things must pass. All things must die.

Quiet, with a house to myself, an odd feeling of exhilaration and loneliness, leafing through parents' drawers and cupboards, looking for intrigue and secrets, evidence of hidden lives. And then that smell. Foul, throat-catching smoke. The smell of fire finding fuel, finding its way, finding momentum and purpose and mass.

Running, silent screaming, iced panic frozen in my throat, choking me. The panic of moments turned. And that sight of flames climbing, licking the wall, breathing and twisting, scraping bright orange claws over cupboard doors, searching for what to consume next. Its noise even more overpowering than the heat, a rush of fury let loose.

I'd left the chip pan on. Now it was building heat and holding it, ready to become something else. I felt the foolishness and thrill of being alone, a fleeting sense of maturity, invincibility, of discovering my own way. And I needed to do something, as every breath was matched by the fire breathing, growing.

Dashing upstairs, every tap on, towels grabbed and plunged into shallow water. And back down, slipping bare heels on wooden stairs, risking a fall, a bone break, and death from swapping air for smoke deep inside me, days before my parents were due to return.

Vague memories of safety videos played at school, of not listening, suppressing laughter at the staged, earnest calls for care. Worrying about friends and what they think, not fire and what it doesn't.

Heat, fuel, oxygen. Heat, fuel, oxygen.

The blaze was rampant, melting the extractor fan over the cooker. Misshapen and ready to fall, weighed down by the raging fire, anger that cannot be contained, that looks to take everything away. Towels flung, the gas turned off, running to the phone, 999 and one word. One word, repeated and repeated. Fire.

Fire is here again now, it is following me. I am sitting up, shivering, the world is taking shape around me. Torch on, but nothing to see. The cottage is intact, unchanged. The grate is cold, there are no signs to match the smell. No smoke, no flame, no shadows cast by creeping, flickering death.

What is happening? I am awake, I'm sure. But there's still that dark acrid smell, deep inside my nose, my lungs. Particles and pollution forcing their way into flesh and blood.

Try to be calm. Try to think of Mum and Dad in a crisis, their clarity, their method. Questions and answers. What is this? Is this real? Where could it be coming from?

Where? Start with yes and no. Fireplace? No. Smoke inside? No. Flames? No. Inside? No. Outside?

Drawing up my jacket collar against the feral bite of winter, it is time for outside. I still hate the darkness, much as Dad did. He wrote about this a lot, and at first I didn't really understand why. But that difference between the softness of city darkness and the blunt hardness of forest darkness has no easy way of being put into words. No words in this language, at least, no words that I have. Here it isn't darkness in the background, it is darkness that seeks you out and overwhelms you.

Unlatch the door, torch peering out, deep breath. It is time for darkness.

Ink black night cloaks me and I'm instantly lost. The smell is worse out here, much worse, invading, but I can't see anything. The torchlight lurches out into the night, but doesn't travel far before dispersing, shrinking, fading. It can show me the ground beneath my feet, but little more.

White light detonates. Lightning, striking the cottage. More fire, the roof slashed through. I cannot breathe.

Silence. Breath-held silence, confused-shock silence.

Lightning again, close, but behind the cottage. Thunder rips the air apart.

Silence and silenced.

Another memory hits, of watching storms as a child, counting the seconds from bright flash to rumble and crash, sitting at my window, curtains parted, gazing wide-eyed at nature's rage. A comforting hand on my shoulder in the dark. Mum's hand.

But what is this? Now it is too near, not far away on a horizon, on an edge that doesn't concern me. I am no longer counting seconds between light and sound, guessing miles, miles away, guessing miles to safety.

There are no seconds and there are no miles. Now I am in the storm. I am the storm.

And I am stuck. The cottage is catching fire, finding its low roar, finding fuel to pick and feed and grow, finding its rhythm. Burning Dad's words, setting him free and cutting me loose from him forever, before I had really found anything. Before I had found him.

Please, please. Dad, Mum, someone, anyone. I can't do this, I can't do this alone. No more and no longer.

I have lost everything, lost it over and over again. All I was left with were words. I need to keep them, protect them. The words can't burn now. They are all I have of him.

I lunge back to the door, leaning in. Smoke and light are spewing out, the boxes of papers smouldering, catching, nurturing flames that quickly grow. Flames that burn Dad's pain, erasing his loss and sad madness. Finally casting away his devil, this nonsense fiction that pursued him to the end. To his anonymous mountain death. He is dead, he is surely dead, and soon I may be too.

There is one small pile of papers on the table, a few steps from the boxes, from the flames. Stupidly, I rush in, grab them, and turn. I fall.

Something has caught my feet, but there is nothing on top of me, nothing in my way. I am held down. The floor is smooth and flat, no table or chair standing between me and the door, between the fire and the air. The smoke is now rushing, filling the room, the noise swelling and swelling. This is a fire that will not stop, that knows no end.

Back to my feet, which are leaden and stuck. This is the smoke, I tell myself, and try again for the door. Sleeve wrapped over mouth and nose, a bundle of papers held inside my jacket, but still I feel held, still I am held. There are hands holding me back. The fire has its own gravity, pulling the world around it in, looking to burn forever until the darkness outside is complete.

One step. Don't breathe. One step. Move, don't breathe, move. Know that it will kill you, it is killing you, the fire wants you to burn. You can see the door, open, night never looked so welcome. Step, step, step, then free. Back out into the icy air, but I can't stop. I must get further away from the cottage. I need more space, I need space to breathe.

Slowly, all I have is slowly, slowly away from the cottage, the night holding me as I stumble, feet jabbing unseen tree roots, awkward steps, tentative, finding my way through this space all over again. Everything is different now, nothing remains. I have walked and run over this ground hundreds of times now, but it is not the same. In darkness everything is new.

Up a little slope, closer to the forest edge, and I can take no more. The ground rises up to take me and I sit, throat charred from smoke, raw, coughing, trying to breathe, nothing left to give. I have a handful of paper memories clutched to my chest, nothing more, as I watch the fire greedily take the roof, crack and smash the window panes, the flames now curling around the door frame. An invitation to death. It wants me back in, beckoning to join it.

I don't notice at first, but I am crying. I've been here for weeks and weeks now and am no closer to Dad, or to Mum, than I was at the start. The cottage meant nothing, but it was my only anchor.

Breathe, breathe. There is always a gap in the panic, always space for a breath. I try to remember this, but it's difficult, my attention keeps being pulled away. I need to be calm, to let go, but the currents are carrying me. Everything is swirling, shifting beneath me, finding directions that are not mine. I am watching the shore disappear. I am becoming the horizon.

Something collapses. More roof, a wall, I can't tell. The forest is filling with smoke now, spreading out between the trees, stretching, searching. I can see less and less, but can still hear the fire, feel it.

Which way? I am trying to breathe, to catch my breath, to find that gap, but it isn't there. Everything is darkness, smoke, and fire, and my own darkness is creeping too. Those positive words I just wrote, and that sense of control I glimpsed, now feel like another pointless story, another fiction. Dad's words are burning in the cottage, and mine are too. Everything is being taken away.

Which way? I need to move somewhere, and move quickly. The car. I must get out, escape, leave forever. The car, behind the cottage.

It isn't far, but the smoke has pushed all the air out of the forest. My eyes and throat are stinging. I'll have to go the long way around, trace a large circle to stay away from the cottage. The heat, the fire, the gravity it has.

Coat still covering mouth and nose, eyes streaming, shadows dancing and playing between the trees. Some weak moonlight melting into the smoke. Light steps, quick, trying to be quiet. Quiet? Why quiet? The forest is noise and heat, and I am keeping quiet?

I'm also half-holding my breath, anticipating something. This is all stupid. Stupid fear and darkness, Dad's fear buried deep inside me too. My fear now. Trace that circle, come all the way around, car, escape. Just keep focused.

Everything is flat now. Layer upon layer of fire, trees, smoke, trees, me. Cards shuffling over each other, then unwrapping, unravelling as I edge further sideways. Fire, trees, smoke, trees, fire. More fire.

The car is burning. The second lightning strike. Both missed me, but both hit. I am stuck. With no escape.

White. Pure bright white, again, then thunder, thick and solid, so loud it punches the breath out of me. I can't see, am not sure what is happening. I need to find a way out of here.

Turning, running, papers spilling from my coat pocket, trying to hold on to them, still running, grabbing at Dad's words, reaching and grabbing again, cold fingertips fumbling, pages strewn across the ground, lying in mud, smoke creeping after us, flooding the world.

Trying to think, to put one thing in front of the other. I need a series of steps to take. They don't feel like mine, but I need to take them anyway. Away, away from the cottage, never to return. There will be nothing to return to after, after all of this.

Moving, moving. Still not seeing straight, haunted by Dad's fear of the darkness, wondering deep down if this is what he was afraid of. Perhaps he was right, perhaps he saw everything correctly. Could I have it all wrong?

No, not that. Thoughts flying now, furious in my brain, sounding over each other, creating my own frenzy, my own whirlwind that can't be seen. Invisible, but real and deadly.

Moving, moving. Trying to avoid tripping, trying to avoid looking back. Feeling the ground, not seeing the ground. Seeing only a world lit from behind, my own shadow flickering around me, cast by the fire. I am moving away, but I am still right here.

Into cold, clean air. Past the forest edge and up. To the big rock, and stop.

Down below, the fire is raging. Both fires. Soon to merge, to come together and spread and spread. They seem smaller now, with distance, but my skin is crawling. I feel sick and confused, angry. Inside I can feel that darkness prowling, searching for something. It needs to feed.

The darkness is the fire and the fire is the darkness. I am starting to burn.

Breathe. Follow the breath. Let it relax, ease, let the world drift around you. I can't. Try counting. Breathe in one, breathe out two. Three, four. To ten. Let thoughts go, don't force them or imagine them leaving, just let go. Here, then not here. But now it is all too much. Find the breath, but I can't. Find the gap, but there is no gap. I am breathing, but I am not in control.

The fire is spreading now. Prowling beyond the cottage, catching the forest all around it, stretching from tree to tree. Alive.

It is coming nearer, seems to be pointing towards me, following. More madness. Breathe, you idiot. Breathe. One, two. Three, four. Let it go. The fire is catching, spreading, not following.

Which way now? The route over the bridge and back to the road, back towards the houses, is blocked by fire and there is no way around it, not without crossing the river. In darkness. Double darkness, above and below water, slick rocks waiting to slip and trip, pull you under, pull you away. I can't turn back, not yet, not until the fire is gone.

People must see this. People must come. My phone? Gone, not here. Back at the house, miles away, on the other side of the fire. Useless out here anyway, and lost. The light of the fire must be carrying, someone must see. Surely.

For now I am alone. I need to stay safe until I can get back down that way, back to the houses. To go up and over would be stupid beyond belief. The next road or house is ten or twenty miles away, over multiple sharp peaks, if I go the right way, and if I don't get lost. This is where people die, every year, some prepared, some less so. Experienced mountaineers, caught out, snow-bound, or slipped and snapped. People die in daylight here, never mind night. People, anonymous people, unnamed people, trying not to think too closely about Dad.

I need to remember not to look at the fire, to turn away, to let my eyes adjust to the darkness, at least a little. I need to find somewhere to rest, somewhere safe, maybe for the whole night. To settle and let calm come back. To hold on.

The darkness is starting to ease. I am seeing more, and hearing more too. The story that was starting is falling away, losing interest in itself. A little calm, a little calmer, but don't chase it. This I've learnt too. There is danger in too much and too little. Tales of darkness and light can both run away with you just as quickly. Both can be wrong.

I have the breath back now, nearly, nearly in control. Breathe in one, breathe out two. To ten, and repeat. It is completely dark, and I have my eyes closed. I am trying to hold on to this moment, nothing before and nothing after. Just breathe, breathe, breathe.

Move, breathe, move. Was that what Mum and Dad used to say? I am confused, panicking still. I am separated from my own memories. I am someone else. I don't want to move just yet, don't know where to. The fire is huge now, filling most of the forest at the bottom of this slope. It is spreading and I can faintly feel the heat even from this distance. The smoke hasn't left me, still clutching to my hair and clothes, the smell alive.

Where to? I can't stay here, sitting on this rock, all night. I am badly dressed, already cold, not enough layers, and a light jacket. No hat, no gloves. If the rain comes, I'll be drenched, frozen, at risk, but there is so little cover that isn't burning. I know this, I know these hills and mountains. I know this wilderness now.

Actually, I don't. I am wrong again, Dad and I are both wrong again. I know them in daytime, not darkness. Remember, remember. I know them in the light when all is clear and open and safe. Now they are something else. Now they have changed, some parts altered, some added, some removed. There may be more and there may be less.

Down doesn't work. Fire circled by a deep river. Straight up doesn't help much either. Too dangerous, no point in climbing and risking, not now. One way to the east traces the edge of the slope, winding up and over, then down through the hollow Dad wrote about in one of the first notes I found. That awful vision, the beginning of his confusions, those echoes and impossibilities. That place I avoid every time I step out of the cottage. The opposite way to the west is much the same, up towards the long ridge and other peaks, then on to the demolished hotel.

And to the outbuilding. The hotel had an outbuilding, long abandoned, boarded up, but still standing and surely dry inside, warmer than here, protected. Somewhere to rest, for now, until daylight returns and the fire is gone. I can break in.

It's a long, dangerous trip. A tough climb, a mile of ridge, then the forest, but out from under the trees there is faint moonlight now, occasionally breaking through the cloud. Turn my back to the fire, eyes adjusted, calmer. If I do not leave here, I will die. Time to move.

The air is colder now. The adrenaline is fading and I am shaking. Movement is good, find a stream to drink from, find that cover, warm up, maybe sleep a little, then soon this will be over. All over. Small step, small step, small step. Enough small steps will bring me to morning.

230

Where is he? Where was he? I feel so lost and angry. He may not have started the fire, burnt the forest, but he brought me here. This past year should have been about Mum, given to her, to remembering and loving and grieving her, but instead it's been all about him, about disappearing. He sent this all up in smoke, sent me up in smoke.

When I set their house on fire, he forgave me. They both did. Another phone call to Mum and Dad but this time no rush back from the mountains, just reassurance, some trust emerging in their uncertain teenager.

I was fine. There'd been a fire engine, an ambulance, hospital checks and tests. No smoke damage, just irritated throat and chest. But during that call I felt a strange tension, of wanting independence and wanting to be held. Of wanting to be an adult and a child, but being caught between the two. That has come back recently, that feeling.

I am some distance above the forest now, following the rough path that runs towards the ridge, but I can still hear the fire faintly crackling, spitting in disgust. The path comes and goes, as do the clouds.

I am moving slowly, occasionally testing the ground ahead with my foot, to check if it will move, if it will hold me, if it has confidence in me. Feeling the uneasy crunch of stones over stones. There are no sheer drops here, or not yet, but the fear of slipping, breaking, and freezing to death is very real. Slowly, slowly. My thin waterproof jacket is pulled up, drawn tight, papers still tucked inside, as heat rushes out of me. One, two. Three, four.

Is it near? Surely it is near. It feels like I've been moving for hours now.

231

Cold, so very, very cold. Cold that cuts. Move, move, move. Trying to pull my hood closer, trying to push my head into the jacket, my hands further and further in, to shrink, to hold any warmth that is left. Getting smaller and smaller, as my body heat bleeds out, as my breaths each freeze, no longer giving anything.

Smaller and smaller. Thinking of Mum, shrunken by illness but still fierce. Eyes as bright as a hawk's.

Moving and moving. Hearing my feet slowly tapping, each step freezing too, movement slowing as everything slows. Feeling the world turn to sound as the moon comes and goes. The sounds of stepping, breathing, burning.

And now up to the ridge, a sheer drop on either side, gritting my teeth.

Feeling the night taking away sensation in my feet and hands, but knowing I cannot stop. Fearfully taking handholds in the rock lit only by moonlight. Doing everything I said I would never do.

This is dangerous, stupid, I know, but I have to leave. Desperation is everything. I have to leave the fire, the cottage, the months and deaths, all of these things. I have to shelter until morning, or I will die. I have to find real shelter to last hours and hours, then I can really leave.

Briefly looking down, the fire has grown bigger and bigger, hardly any of the forest not burning now. So big it has stretched to the firebreak lines, the straight cuts through the woods that pattern everything around here. A precaution, but one that was needed tonight.

Rocks slip under me. Distracted, stupid, heart in throat. Grab, claw, reach, hold anything. I can't fall. Fingernails skip over rock cracks, feet kick into nothing.

Kicking, kicking, and stopped. A knee jammed against an edge, an elbow and arm wedged on the other side. Hands pushing out, the other leg forcing up, hands frantic, pulling, scrabbling, hauling over. I can hear myself coughing, grunting, swearing.

I shouldn't have looked. Stay focused, stay focused.

There is further to go.

And after a long time, after teetering on that edge, hunched over, raw hands clawing, feet tentatively reaching for cracks that will hold, that might hold, then the ridge starts to twist and flatten.

Standing properly now, walking in stutters, then more smoothly. The loose stones give way to firmer, surer ground. Up and over. Now to the next forest, the forest in darkness, remembering not to be pulled away by the curving slope of the hill. Remembering that straight line, connecting the ridge to the peak far, far away that I can no longer see. The hotel is in between.

Holding on to fear, not letting it run away. Knowing that each step is taking me closer, closer to a chance of a roof and walls. To hiding from the night until it too has passed.

The trees scratch at my arms and eyes. I stumble on. In the night it is all sound.

The trees thin, freeing me of the face-slapping branches. The moon-light returns, then paving and a silhouette of the hotel.

Far away there are sirens now, tiny, shrill. I can imagine their noise drowned by the fire, completely and utterly lost.

This is the hotel, it definitely is, but it can't be. It stands solid and unmoved. Too solid.

I am in the same place, I have travelled the same torturous journey. The huge front wall is still here, the side walls and the outbuilding too, but now there is so much more. It's not the demolished ruin I found before, emptied and hollow, walls standing open-armed and alone. It is complete again.

It is huge and intact, but it can't be. Four or five floors, hundreds of rooms, rounded turrets crowning each corner.

I must be on the front terrace, in front of grand windows that hide dining rooms and parlours with endless views, looking out on a perfect, contained wilderness. Another beautiful fiction, packaged and served.

Back in its prime it would have been painted white, starkly, aggressively white, announcing itself far across the glen, visible from all the mountaintops, dominating nature, sharp against the bright greens of summer and the orange grasses and bracken of autumn's end. It said that nothing is too wild, too beautiful to be contained. It said that the mess and sprawl is all here to be taken, to be picked from, to be turned into a menu of delights for rich men and women to enjoy.

There is the arched stone entrance, protecting anyone who arrived from the rain and the wind. Far away I can see the light and smoke escaping from the fire, a false sunset in the middle of the night, filling the sky behind the ridge.

234

I am warmer now, so can afford to sit for a little while before trying to break in, take cover, and rest in the darkness. I can sit on the steps to try and work this out, but I have so little energy for puzzles and confusion, for connecting what doesn't connect. There are walls and a roof. That might have to be enough for now.

The darkness is no longer so intimidating and absolute. Now it has a texture. My fear is contained, unlike Dad's, or is at least so numb as to be unrecognisable. I feel strong, capable, confident after getting away, after surviving my terrifying late-night climb across the mountain. Things I have done and should not have done. There is a whisper of a story starting, but it fades. Not to run away with that confidence, but to let it sit, untouched, unnoticed. Sit with it, aware, but not needing or craving it.

Tonight is the end to all this. I was spinning in circles, but now I am clear. There are no answers, so I need to be relaxed about that. Now there is only grief and confusion, and time. I need more time, time away from all of this. I have been staring straight at grief for months now. No wonder I can't see anything clearly.

Part of moving on might be learning that I can't finish everything. That to not understand doesn't mean I must keep trying, endlessly, immovably. Choosing to walk away is its own finish line. Even if what I leave behind is partial, incomplete, or even broken, now is the time to move.

Move, breathe, move. The chilled air is getting to me again, so I must get inside. Everything is different now. Everything is new. Give up, and let it go. Start again. Breathe in, breathe out. I just need a way in, some loose chipboard covering a window or doorway, to prise at with cracked, bleeding fingertips, to work loose, but each panel I try is firmly stuck down. They are all spray-painted with the name of a security or construction company, a warning that means nothing to me.

The hotel does not want to be opened, it is resisting. The outbuilding is too. And it's quickly getting colder. I'm breathing clouds into my hands, wishing for gloves, rubbing fingers together furiously, even though I know I should keep them close to my body, under my clothes, under my arms. But I need to get in soon. Numbing slowly, arms, legs, body. It's hard to come back when the ice properly sets in your blood and in your bones.

The irony. Back behind the ridge is a fire the size of a housing estate, while here the cold is chasing me, gradually working into me, as I fail to find any way in. A fire would help, a fire here, but I have nothing to start one with. I am surrounded by the cold, closing in and closing in.

Around another corner, to the back of the hotel. It is quieter here, muffling the distant panic and terror of the forest fire. Darker, moonlight hiding now. Fewer windows, less to look out upon, a firmly shut doorway. The back of the hotel isn't flat, it has edges and alcoves, staircases dropping down to service quarters. Each door and window is firm and I can't find anything to smash through the chipboard, or wrench it open. Anything dangerous or interesting has been long since taken by local teenagers, picking the hotel carcass clean.

A few steps down I see another doorway, uncovered. The door handle briefly shines as the moon escapes through the clouds. The hotel stretches and shifts in the light, and the flat wall seems to ripple, to shiver and breathe. It gains depth, letting the door unlock. Letting it move. I really am tired now. Ridiculous nonsense, surely. It must be.

But this door does open. Hinges rusted from years of rain and neglect, even though they cannot be, even though this was all demolished and gone just a few days ago. Metal biting metal. Screeching, slowly, loudly. It only opens a little, but I can squeeze inside, to be warm enough to last until tomorrow.

Dad would truly hate this. The darkness inside is absolute. This is totally different from the rich, shifting night outside, occasionally lit brilliantly by the moon but still never dark enough not to cope. It is so dark inside it doesn't feel like the same thing at all.

To have a torch. My torch? Not here, dropped somewhere, lost now too. No use thinking like that – to have a fire, a phone, another life. To get away, to have never come here at all. To have them both still, or at least a death then a death, not a death then chaos. To have no talk of devils. To have no fires, burning, following me.

Breathe.

The smell is thick. Damp, must, stale air so close it touches you, forces its way down your throat.

There is no light, and there is no sound. Either would terrify me now. I am stepping with each breath, tracing a line along one wall with my frozen fingers, creeping deeper inside. I'm not sure what there is to find in the darkness, but there is comfort in movement. There is warmth.

These could be kitchen corridors, staff bedrooms, anything. I have no idea, but I take a breath with each step. I can't walk all night, but for now it is providing almost enough comfort to keep everything together. Just enough distraction. One night, then over, then away. Then to start again.

My fingertips are tracing wooden panels. I imagine rich oak, swirling and knotted, deeply and darkly stained. I can feel their vertical edges, the thin gaps between, at regular intervals. With each step my fingers run over three or four grooves, bumping lightly, thinking of trains crossing bridges and regular, comforting rhythms.

The wall ends at a doorway. Both edges, left and right, have now stopped. A corridor leading to, or leading away. A metal door handle, round, cold, turning. The door, heavy and huge, slowly opens.

From darkness to darkness, but the sounds of my footsteps have changed. Tight and closed in the corridor, now they echo, spread, and explore. I imagine an expansive and tall room, panelled to its high ceiling, a grand space for whisky and smoking. For men. A room for raging fires, for dead animal heads hung at height. For noise and tinkling glass and finest silver scraping over white china. It could be anything, but to me, now, this is what it is. A room built for heat, comfort, loud congratulation, now frozen to the touch.

The air is clearer here too. Perhaps there are fireplaces connecting to chimneys, letting the fresh air in? Breathing in and breathing out.

A noise. I jump, startled. Mice? Rats? Scraping and scratching inside walls? It must be, but in the darkness my mind is racing. My heartbeat.

I need to breathe, to hold on. Tonight I just need to stay inside, stay here long enough that the fire dies, the night dies, the morning begins again. To wait for brightness. Brightness always comes.

Settling again, calming, the rodents in the walls now escaped somewhere else. I sit, on the floor, feeling the room's heavy loneliness. The darkness is so thick and I am so exhausted that my eyes are not adjusting at all. I can picture a fiction of a banquet hall, but I could be in a restaurant or a giant food store. It could be either of these or something else entirely, but it is dry. It is enough.

The floor is cold and hard. I lie down, try to rest, hoping that time will move on without me, carry me in sleep to a new morning. To afterwards. But I can't sleep, it's too hard, too uncomfortable. I drag myself to my feet and track around the room, imagining a grid of lines on the floor, repeating squares to divide up this huge space, stepping along them, trying to find furniture, or even walls, but nothing. No walls, no doorway. Slowly stepping, always anticipating bumping into something unseen, wincing in anticipation of pain that does not come.

Step forward ten paces. Nothing. Back ten paces. Right ten paces. Left. Forward twenty paces, back, right, left. Trying to keep the grid, to keep focused, to hold on to one location that is mine, that I can keep, protect, come back to. A centre. But still nothing. Step forward thirty paces, turn around. Forty paces, turn around. Walking a little faster now, less fearful of surprise and pain, but closer to panic.

Nothing. Still no walls, no edges, no furniture. This must be a ballroom, some kind of Highland cathedral, empty for years and years and years. Except it wasn't. It was demolished, but it is here now. I am starting to unravel, but have to try and hold on. Cold outside, cold inside, that familiar ice throat choke starting, breaths shallowing and skipping. I am inside, dry, warmer than outside, I tell myself. I think I hear rain now too. Just wait here, inside, until morning. Tell yourself to wait.

Imagine looking back on this. Not a story to tell, to share with warmth and humour, but a hidden, secret relief that this is all behind me, in the past, a moment that keeps shrinking until it disappears. This will pass, this must pass.

Noise, again. Louder. Rats, surely.

Thinking of homes where rodents got in, the outside coming through to the inside, scratching in the walls as you tried to sleep, as you tried to pretend it wasn't happening.

What is that? Not scratching, not scurrying. A different sound, a different texture, vanishing in this vast space, whatever this room is. For a moment I think I'm outside, but I check myself. I came through that door, that corridor, then here. That suffocating smell, then running fingertips over wooden panels, then here. Still here.

And noise. Far away, I think. The fire? It can't be. It was miles away, behind the ridge, hemmed in by the firebreak lines and the river. The noise is something else, somewhere else. Closer.

I am starting to really panic. I know this, I see this, I can stop this. I need to stop. To stop quickly. Breathe in, breathe out. One night to get through, then done. Tell yourself. A few hours, light will creep in, will trace the edges of this room, will give it shape and walls and ceiling. To put an to end to the threat of imagination. To find a way back out again.

Hold on to the breath, feel it drawing in, chest rising, notice where the motion is. Let the ice melt, the breath deepen and slow. How does it feel? Warm, cool? Calm or stuttering? Feel the breath leave, the muscles relaxing, the chest falling. And repeat and repeat and repeat. How many breaths until morning? How many breaths in a life?

I hear Dad's words, calling to me. Some of the calm, loving messages, some of the stranger ones too. I try to block out the notes that came alive and spoke directly to me and to themselves. To block out that stupid obsession with devils, all of his cruel hallucinations, surely hallucinations, and then at the end his final push. To exhaustion, to collapse, to a pointless death, somewhere near here. His quest for someone who could never be found. Looking until he was lost too.

I'm sitting again, but can't remember sitting down. No matter. For a moment I am completely calm. An acceptance washes over me. This is it, for now. I am fine. I have to be. Not freezing, not wet, not trapped by flames. All this will pass. Soon it will pass. Don't panic, don't let panic start panic. How many breaths until morning?

But something. That noise, repeating, but changed. Bigger, deeper. And a smell. Was that there before? There is dampness, stale air, mould, and must. I'm imagining again, I think, senses playing with me, my brain looking for things that aren't here. Filling in the darkness. Let it go, back to the breath. Calm and calm. Breathe in, breathe out. And again.

No. Not here too.

Smoke.

It is real. There is fire, somewhere, somewhere near.

There can't be, but there is.

Somewhere inside, but not seen in the darkness. Still everything is ink, flat, no walls, nothing to see. But smell. Distant, I think, but not far, far away. Part of the building, invading every space. The hotel is on fire.

Calm. Calm now. I need to hold on to myself. Standing again. Remember you came in here, there is a way out. No room can be endless. You can keep walking to an edge, follow it, repeat and repeat. Fingertips in the darkness. Soon there will be a door, back out again, that corridor, those steps up, the clean air of night. The brightness of the moon.

But don't panic. It is here but not here yet. Closing, not close. I have lost all bearing, no sense of which way I came in. Walk forward, count the steps. Slowly, methodically. Breathe. Listen to the noise, the fire. Is it changing? Nearing?

Count the steps. To thirty, thirty-one. Nothing. Flat floor, no stairs, no tables, no furniture. No walls. To forty-nine, fifty, fifty-one. How long is a step? How long is a room? To sixty-five, sixty-six. This can't make sense. Am I walking in circles? I can't be. Keep going. Hold the nerve. To eighty-seven, eighty-eight, eighty-nine. Don't panic. Don't. To one hundred and one, one hundred and two, one hundred and three.

Breathe, you idiot. Stop for a moment, breathe in, breathe out. Repeat and repeat. Whatever is burning is still far away. There is nothing to see, just that hot, thick smell seeking you out, the noise threatening. Don't let the story start, don't let it take you away. Find the gap. There is always a gap, space for a breath. Space for thinking to stop.

How long is a room?

The noise. I can hear the old building aching and creaking, frozen wood warming up long before the fire envelops it. Expanding, waking. Waking only to die.

Light. All light. The room explodes into life. From black to white in a moment, but silent. No noise. No noise at first, but starting now. A storm inside these walls. My confusion is painfully slow, then it is all speed.

A huge fireplace, a grand hall. Gold-framed portraits of men. Dead animal heads glaring. Where did one hundred steps go? This is not the room. Dark again.

Lightning? Here? Flashes of light now, screaming in. The room has turned. I have turned. Fireplace now behind me. Spinning around. Fire pouring out from it, washed down the chimney. Dark again.

I am Dad. I am hallucinating. This is not here and not real.

Flashing again. Bright. Fading, to dark, fingers reaching up the walls.

At the centre, a shape.

I am not alone in this room.

243

NO. NOT ALONE

Dad's devil is here.

Fire, flames casting shapes, bringing back the walls, making this room a room again. Door? Door? Running away. Away first, then out, then away and away.

Run, run, run.

Door.

Door?

Smaller than before, but a door. There are no others. This is not the room. Not the door. Flung, opened, running. Corridor and corridor, light fading. Light chasing.

Corridor and corridor. Turning, turning. Almost dark again, light at my back, but I can't slow, can't stop.

Door again. To outside?

To the room, the same room. Back again. Fire and shape and fireplace.

This can't be. It can't.

NOT ALONE

Run.

Running, running, scraping elbows, arms, edges, hot now, fire seeking me out, clawing for lungs. Air inside swapped for smoke. Pushing out life and light.

Dark. Running. Stumble, fall, hit. Scream and stand and run and run.

HUNTING

Words felt, not heard. No sound but the fire.

Fire has followed me here. I prayed for warmth and here it is. This is what I get. This is what I deserve.

Feeling panic build, feeling a vicious story build, as I try to unpick the way I came in. The hotel rippled in the moonlight and let me in, now it has closed again. Filling itself with smoke, trying to fill me with smoke.

Darkness, scared of the darkness, Dad's fear and my fear, and no one to hold me, to stop this, to tell me it will all be over soon. It will. Will it?

Scrabbling at corridor walls, feeling nothing but warming wooden panels and peeling wallpaper. No other doors, no other way to go. Gasping and spluttering in dank mouldy air.

Frantic now, fast now.

Forward, but forward brings me back again, back to what I am trying to leave, what I want to find and want to forget.

Dad, surely dead, in these mountains. Mum, dead, not in these mountains.

Everything is darkness. Everything is death.

I can stop now, right now.

I can stop and wait and decide that it is all hopeless. Maybe now is time, maybe there is no time.

WAITING

WAITING

TIME WAITS

Dad's devil is still here.

No, no, no, no, no. Find the fight again. I will not wait for you. I will not look in your eyes, or let you look in mine.

LOOK

LOOKING

Look away from that jagged, twisted shape. Look beyond what you can see, know there is more, even if it is not here, even if it is not now.

I feel heat building, heat inside and outside. The fire and my despair, calling to each other. Everything burning.

But I will not, cannot. Forward, forward. There must be a way, there must be other ways.

Finding, finding, finding. Finding a door, a wall, an edge, a moment to step through and beyond. I can find it. I will not stop.

STOPPING

STOPPING

EASY

REST

I will not stop. I will not listen.

246

I know I am in movement, I am made of movement. If I stop, I die.

The smoke building and building, its smell, its threat, remembering how the heat of fire pushes smoke up, clinging to the ceiling, forcing clean, cold air down, pushing it out.

Should I run or should I crawl? I want to run, always want to run, but balancing speed and escape with choking and death.

Not knowing, again not knowing. All the things I do not know.

And suddenly from hot to cold, darkness to moon.

Back outside again, somehow outside. Were there steps, doors, more corridors?

The hotel is different again, walls leaning, warped. Tricks of the light. Must be tricks of the light. Hallucinations. Must be.

But the fire is real. I must run.

There is hard ground, gravel and paving washed by moonlight, clouds above fading in and fading out. There's enough light to see, to move, to run.

Back the way I came. Turning, my back to the hotel, the new fire. I wished for fire, for warmth, but not this, never this. Sprinting, no breath, no breath. Stop. Remember. There are miles and miles to go. Run to run all night.

Everything I want turns to ruin.

Again. Off the hard ground, into the forest, branches stinging face and arms, hurting but not slowing, back to crunching stone, then to a thin track, a new track, hard, smooth, twisting and turning. Running on a snake's back.

Running away, but not sure where. To be away, I have to be away. I should be coming towards the ridge, but it isn't here. Just keep going.

I must be being pulled down the other slope, where I got lost when I first failed to find the hotel that can't be but is. I am lost again, but running, running, running. To be away and away.

Some distance. I want to stop but can't stop. I need to run and run. Over on the other side of the mountain the forest is raging, lighting the sky orange above me, above us.

Turn. The hotel is burning now too, all-consuming, all to be consumed. After this there will be nothing. The world will be empty.

Start again. To run. Moving is safe, stopping is not. Legs hard and heavy now, cold through, muscles need to move and thaw. To warm. To get blood flowing. More and more.

That noise, thick and heavy, hanging over me. Not burning, more than that.

The noise of death.

Stop and turn. I am running. From what? Stories spinning, overtaking me. Telling and telling and telling. I hear death, but see?

SEE ME

Run run run run run run run

That shape, what Dad saw, that message. Real, real, and real.

248

Real and here and now.

Real and here and me.

Run.

To run all night. To run forever. I must keep going. I must.

Where doesn't matter. Just keep going.

I am lost, but must lose it, that evil shape.

There is no stopping, there is no end.

This is it. This is now. These stupid months, real and real.

Skip, jump, slide. Track disappears, scree, stones stumbling, back to track.

Where doesn't matter.

Just keep going.

Move, breathe, move.

Running from it, a devil, the Devil. Running, running, running.

Not a story, just fire and death.

There are no stories now.

Running running running

Minutes, miles, hours, sweating, screaming, running. Run and run. Run until morning sun.

Morning sun brightness

Spinning spinning spinning

Real stories? All real? Notes and notes, now fire. Fire and lightning and run.

Thousands of pieces of fire.

Follow the track, over crests and rises, views lost to darkness, moonlight, blessed moonlight. Moonlight is enough.

Turning in and out, feeling the land bucking, wanting rid of this, wanting rid of me, writhing and hurting and no.

Keep going.

I am hurting. I am not now, not this.

I am not here, he is not here, Dad and Mum, dead and dead, and I am, I will be, but not yet.

I am here and life and living.

I must not stop, I must find another way.

Which way? No matter, but forward and forward.

Keep going forward, to find where forward is, where it could be.

And the hollow, back to the hollow, the sharp sides and stunted trees. Where Dad met the Devil.

How? It's been miles and miles, hours and hours. I'm on the wrong side of the ridge, the wrong side of the mountain. It can't be here, but it is.

I ran away. But I'm slipping over the edge, tumbling down into the hollow, back to that note that was so easily cast away, dismissed as not real.

Dad stood here. Dad fell apart here. This is where he imagined all of his impossible horrors.

This is where I've avoided and avoided.

HERE

No. Not here.

Can't be here. Can't be real.

Trapped and trapped.

HERE

Breathe.

There is always a gap to breathe

breathe breathe breathe

this is a panic attack and you know that

this is not real and you know that

there is no devil Devil watching waiting burning finding chasing just you and the mountain

there is moonlight there is moonlight there is moonlight

breathe breathe breathe

there must be more more than this

breathe breathe breathe

forward forward forward

and forward and finding and now and now

this is not me I am not this thing I am not my sadness my grief my depression I am not my darkness

Iamnotmydarkness

I am not my darkness

I am not my darkness.

Breathe. Breathe. Breathe.

This is a panic attack and this is not real.

I am not my darkness.

I am not running because I am not being chased.

I will turn and face you.

I will turn, now, and I will stop time.

TURN

I am not my darkness and I am not you.

I am the gap between breaths. My breath.

Turn.

TURN

I will stare into your eyes and watch you fade, the fire lull, the smoke settle.

I am not my darkness.

Breathe.

Turn.

TURN

You may be the Devil, my devil, but you are not me and I am not my darkness.

I am Dad and Mum and light.

I am light and you are no more.

I am not my darkness.

Turn.

TURN

I am not story, or silence. I am me and me.

I am forward and finding, I am now.

I am not my darkness.

Turn.

TURN

Turn to fire, total fire, filling the sky, the land, everything. All is red and black and orange, and red and black and smoke.

All is heat, shimmer, burning air.

I am not my darkness.

I have run enough, run away, hidden. I have slipped through years, spinning stories, crafting and creating the me of me. A me of stories, of sad stories, of failure and blame. Written, then real. Written, then me.

I am not my darkness, am not your darkness. I am not your fire, your fury, whatever the you of you.

You may be real, but you are not.

QUIET VOICE

LISTEN

No. This is the story that I've written and written and written, written in blood and muscle, written in years. Carved deep down within me, hidden and unknown. Within me but not me.

LISTEN

THIS IS YOU

I AM YOU

LISTEN OR BURN

TIME NO MORE

254

I will tell my own story.

I am not my darkness.

QUIET

QUIET VOICE

YOUR VOICE

And I close my eyes and scream to the night.

I am not my darkness, or yours.

Listen to me.

Now I breathe.

I am the gap between breaths, and I am always here.

Now is now is now. Now is mine.

Darkness, brightness, now.

Dawn

They are gone now, they really are.

Mum's death I never doubted. I felt the light in the crematorium, the chill outside. I still hear her in birdsong, remembering her glow in nature, her knowledge of it, all that we shared.

Dad's death is new, Dad's death is now. I had been grieving and hoping, both at the same time, for so long. Moving and standing still. Torn by this, feeling myself stretched, always on edge, always uncomfortable.

But no, those aren't the right words. More like the world being separated so slowly that no one else notices, no one but you. That you are holding the edges of reality in your hands, every muscle tensed against what will happen, what must happen, that you are in between and gradually being torn apart.

To smile when you are being ripped in two, to find conversation and small talk, to commute, to work, to laugh and love. None of these things can be, none of these things are possible, but we all do them.

It has ended. He is nowhere. He is not here.

He will not be found, or not found as I want him to be found. I try not to think of what really happened, of his own ending. Not a hospital ending, but a mountain terror ending. Not loved ones and machines and buzzing strip lights, but cold and dark and alone. Convinced he was not alone, but alone, even more so in the madness.

This is the end.

This is the end, but I can't stop.

You are here now.

It is light outside, light holding possibility and promise. Light that gives.

This is you and this is now.

Hold the moment.

7.55am. Nearly dawn.

There is nothing, and there is everything. The cottage is collapsed, deflated, smoke still slowly rolling from the hot remains, with tiny clouds of paper ash stirred as the wind kicks and turns. Dad's memories caught in mid-air with nowhere to go.

I can't quite understand what happened, what I really saw. I am deeply confused. My legs hurt beyond any hill climb or long run, beyond any charity marathon of dragging my feet over relentless tarmac. My muscles have been stripped, carved, and returned to me. I am exhausted beyond words. Empty.

But alive. Alive, breathing, grateful. I have some calmness too, some peace. Still frayed, tense, but the anger has gone. It may come back but, for now, it is gone.

There was a fire, two fires at least, but beyond that I don't know. I'm not sure about the hotel, its terror and impossibilities. Maybe that can come later, much later. I'm not sure how that could be, or what it was, what I saw up there. The heat and noise, the darkness shifting around me, that shape framed by flame. Dad's devil born from his terrified pages into the world.

I am too tired to know anything.

Except this: I am not my darkness.

What next? Everything has passed. They are both dead, there were no miracles, no secrets in caves, no mysteries revealed in the passing light. No miracles, but still I am saved. No, that sounds stupid. Pious. A little empty, and imprecise too.

Not saved, but something. Something like starting again, but not that either.

I am not my darkness, or any other darkness. There is darkness, real and painful, and it is everywhere. But there are beauty and light too, and there are choices.

Before, I never saw the choices.

Between everything and everything there is a gap, a moment so small you let it disappear. As you rush and panic, flying from distraction to distraction, these spaces collapse. Gaps no more. But slow, slow, slow, and they begin to appear, to bud and blossom. Possibilities open up, where a new comfort and ease can grow.

When I was young I remember watching the ripples on a pond near our home. Patterns that spread and overlap as the wind stirs, carries, or flattens them. An endless movement, on top of still water beneath. Before, all I noticed was the restless surface.

I am the gap between breaths, or at least I try to be. This will take time, all the time I have and more. I try to lie at the bottom of the pond, to be the calm waters below, where the ripples never reach. Watching them brush the water, but knowing that they will pass.

And the papers. I managed to save some, zipped tight inside my jacket. Of the thousands and thousands I now have a dozen or so pages, but these are enough.

I sit, back at the big rock again, and smooth out the paper.

They feel like hidden pages, words I never found before. And I am in these words.

I remember holding you for the first time. Someone had told me to treasure that moment, to be prepared for it, to know it, to grab it before it passes.

You didn't want to come into the world. Mum was in labour for days, days of pain and panic, starting and stopping, and then everything happened.

262

It was summer, late, as night slips into morning. The windows were open, letting cool air in, but also birdsong. That beautiful mismatched choir, welcoming the day, welcoming you to us. It had also rained. I remember that smell.

And I held you, remembering to remember. You were tiny, perfect, mewling, nuzzling. Cleaned, naked, at the start of your own story. Eyes closed, soft fingertips pawing at my shoulder. The most gentle, imperceptible sensation you could imagine.

I think I had wanted to cut the cord, a symbol, another story people tell. But in the final moments of professional rush, of our panic, of a fading heartbeat and umbilical cord around your neck, of no breath, of Mum needing help quickly, that had been lost.

Mum looked at me, in her pain, exhaustion, joy. We shared a world in that look. A new world, just about to start.

It's amazing how many of the moments people tell you matter don't. How their story isn't yours, and never should be.

But holding you mattered.

There are moments that mean too much, that feel too big and weighty to describe. Moments of hurt and loss, or creation and achievement. Complex and overwhelming.

This was that, but it was something else too. Something so pure and simple. Weightless.

It didn't last long, as you needed to be given back, wrapped, checked again, measured, recorded. To have your existence timed, dated, made official.

But that was the greatest moment of my life. Nothing can take that from me, from us. We two, we three, we shared in that moment, we made that moment.

It isn't summer today, but something stirred this memory. Perhaps the sunlight, warm on my skin, or birdsong. Birdsong that she loved so much.

There is light, and maybe that is all we ever need.

8.07am. Dawning.

There was fire, and now there is not. There were fire engines, rushing and struggling, and then brutal, torrential rain.

Fire and water turning to steam, the forest boiling, then slowly, slowly extinguished.

I sheltered as best I could under a rocky outcrop, shielded from the wind as it blew the rain over and down, but cold and cold and cold.

Hours passed, the moon slipped back behind clouds, the light of the fire ebbed. I listened to the wind and rain, to the fire crackling, spitting, and failing, its anger fading to frustration, to a low, hissing collapse.

The dawn came then, slowly, a glory of pinks that unfolded into shining gold. A sky so intense you could feel it, almost hear it.

I had kept moving throughout the night, through the storm, as best I could under my tiny roof of rock, my partial shade and shelter. Jumping, stretching, pacing, turning, anything to create some heat.

Making heat, losing heat, over and over, knowing that this would soon be over, that the night was nearly over.

Watching that sky, those colours of winter sunrise that feel like they belong nowhere else, that arrive and pass so quickly as to be unseen.

I moved through the night, and am here now. The hotel? Hollow? Devil? I could go back and look later, but I won't. I saw what I saw, felt what I felt. Whatever they can be, or could be, they were. I've run on and through and beyond them. There is nothing to run away from any more.

I could move, I could get to the car. But no, the car burnt too. The fire brigade will need to take me home again.

I will leave, but not quite yet.

For now I just want to sit, to watch the ruined forest below, decades and centuries disfigured.

To breathe, to find those spaces, and to look at the last few notes I have left.

Know this: you never pushed me away.

We are gone and we are both here.

You were always here, you just didn't know where to look.

The Devil hid you from you but is no more.

8.51am. Bright.

Again, another impossible note, another reply from nowhere. This happened before, but now I just move on, keep moving. If I can't change it, or explain it, I can't worry about it. I should be shocked, but am not.

I am broken and need to heal, have been burnt and need to grow again, but I don't think that is all. I have already moved on, though to where I'm not entirely sure.

All that matters is wherever I was stuck before, sucked down into the earth by worry, anger, by much worse, I have clawed out. Now I am free.

And this is it. Time to leave, to start again, but this time with kindness, not with weight and worry, and certainly without expectation. To try and move without anticipating, self-sabotaging, spinning stories that can't be achieved, to attack, demean, humiliate myself when I surely fail to fulfil them. To start again.

To be free, to move, to be stuck in the ground no longer.

This is the ultimate feeling during a run, often fleeting, glimpsed, of moving without effort. Of flow. When your brain slows and stops, as your body glides, as your breath merges with the wind and everything eases. Something so beautiful, so precious that you have to hold it carefully, for fear of crushing or losing it.

This is something you might never feel, or experience only once or twice in a lifetime.

I am holding it now, but for the first time without moving. I am sitting, I am breathing calmly. I am aware of everything around me but am not distracted, concerned, worried about a thing. I can't look too closely or this moment will disappear, but I know this is it.

I watch this feeling from the corner of my eye, a tiny, shy creature twitching for a predator, alert, ready to leap back into the forest and never to be seen again, to be no more than a memory. I watch, silently, gently, joyfully, but breathing it all in.

I am breath, I am movement, I am not my darkness. I am not that voice.

I am not those stories, fantasies of achievement and failure, told and given, forced and received, distorted and distorting. I am the space between, the gap.

This is my story to tell, and it is told in steps and breaths.

It is a story of love.

It is simple and light.

It is kind, and it begins now.

Acknowledgements

I've just watched Alan Cumming in *Burn*, an incredible National Theatre of Scotland production exploring the life of Robert Burns through dance and theatre. Near the end he declares, "And still my motto is, I dare!" That struck a chord with me.

These are the people who allowed me to dare to write this book. My very sincere thanks to you all.

Firstly, my beautiful, hilarious, and kind wife and daughter, Elaine and Niamh. You are both beyond wonderful. You bring me such joy and strength every day. I've never laughed so much in my entire life, and I don't know what I'd do without you both. Sorry I hid this book from you until it was finished!

To my parents, Jenni and Peter, for all of your love and support, and for teaching me never to accept the world as it is given to you. From introducing me to running to moving to Orkney for a summer, you've shown me the thrill of actively changing the world around you – and the rewards of hard work and patience.

To my sisters, Helen and Sally, for your love, laughter, and support. To your wonderful husbands, Chris and Matthew, for your kindness and strength. And to your glorious children, Lyla and Theo, and Lewis, for being the very best of your already fabulous parents.

To my closest friend, Dom Beaumont, for over 25 years of trouble-making and always being there for me. We've both come a long way. To my oldest friend, Dave Smith, for your relentless energy and creativity. Though we never did build that hovercraft, did we? It's been a huge pleasure watching both of your families grow.

To my in-laws, Brian and Joyce, for welcoming me into your family and for all of your support for ours. And for taking us to Glen Coe for the holiday that sparked the idea for this book in the first place!

To all of my extended family, both those who are with us and those we've lost.

This book would not have been possible without so many people. Firstly, the incredible videogame designer Simon Meek for introducing me to Jenny Todd, the most remarkable agent and hilarious partner-in-crime I could hope for. Thank you, Jenny, for changing my life – I will always be grateful to you. To everyone at my publisher HarperNorth, particularly my brilliant, compassionate, fearless editor Daisy Watt who took a risk on me and guided the text with the utmost care as it grew and developed, and Alice Murphy-Pyle for all of your wonderful promotional creativity.

Fray also wouldn't have happened without Max Porter and George Saunders, although neither of them had any idea of this at the time.

Reading *Lanny* and *Lincoln in the Bardo* each gave me the strength to continue with my writing at my lowest moments, vividly reassured that beautiful, risk-taking literature was possible. You taught me to keep working and find what was different about my writing – and then to celebrate that.

There are so many other colleagues who have sparked my creativity without knowing it – from their direct support for me, or just from seeing them thrive and take their own risks.

To Phil Long and Jane Ferguson for giving me the chance to join V&A Dundee years before it opened. To my professional brother and sister, Jamie Gray and Tara Wainwright, for our years working together and looking out for each other. To Jennie Patterson for your friendship and support through both tough and exhilarating times. To Olivia Rickman for your creativity and sound advice. To all of my colleagues at V&A Dundee and V&A South Kensington who are such a joy.

To Creative Scotland who are funding me to take a sabbatical to write my second novel, focused on autism, and to everyone at V&A Dundee who has supported me stepping away for a year. To Malath Abbas and Kristina Johansen Seznec for your advice and support in starting that next chapter.

To Colin Anderson, a dear friend and mentor, and everyone else working in Dundee's videogames sector. To everyone I previously worked with at Abertay University who gave me their friendship and helped my confidence grow. To all the designers I've had the pleasure to work with and to the endlessly creative people of Dundee, a truly beautiful and exciting city. Whether you make videogames or jewellery, please know that your creativity and passion breed creativity in others. What you do matters.

To all the journalists, media professionals, photographers, and film-makers I've had the honour of working with over the years. I've been thrilled to collaborate with you all. To Julie Howden, Shahbaz Majeed, and Ross Fraser McLean for wonderful book-related photography. Special thanks to the incomparably talented and thoughtful film-makers Dougie Walker and Brian Ross of STROMA Films. You are the best.

Finally, running has given me strength again and again. To everyone I've ever trained with and raced with, your dedication and tenacity are an inspiration. To my childhood club, Morpeth Harriers, especially Jim Alder and the late, great Tony Ward. And to everyone at Edinburgh University Athletics Club, Edinburgh AC, and Dundee Hawkhill Harriers. Running clubs change lives. It's as simple as that.

And to you, dear reader. Thank you for everything you've brought to this book.

This should be a beginning, not an end. What do you dare?

Chris Carse Wilson. Scotland, August 2021.

Harper North

would like to thank the following staff and contributors for their involvement in making this book a reality:

Hannah Avery	Jean-Marie Kelly
Fionnuala Barrett	Taslima Khatun
Claire Boal	Sammy Luton
Ciara Briggs	Oliver Malcolm
Sarah Burke	Alice Murphy-Pyle
Jonathan de Peyer	Adam Murray
Anna Derkacz	Genevieve Pegg
Tom Dunstan	Agnes Rigou
Kate Elton	Angela Snowden
Simon Gerratt	Florence Shepherd
Monica Green	Eleanor Slater
Natassa Hadjinicolaou	Emma Sullivan
CJ Harter	Katrina Troy
Megan Jones	Daisy Watt

For more unmissable reads,
sign up to the HarperNorth newsletter at
www.harpernorth.co.uk

or find us on Twitter at
@HarperNorthUK

Harper
North